LOVE BY DESIGN

LOVE BY DESIGN

A CYPRESSVILLE NOVEL

KRISTEN TASSIN

ISBN 978-1-7374589-2-0 (eBook)

ISBN 978-1-7374589-3-7 (paperback)

The characters and events in this book are fictitious. Any similar to real persons, living or dead, is coincidental and not intended by the author.

Editor | Shona McLaren

Editor | Nathan Winfrey

Cover design | KTK Designs

❀ Created with Vellum

For Emily and Rachel

CHAPTER ONE

*J*enna parked her car in front of her monogram shop and started walking toward the park. The early morning sun barely showed behind the clouds. Fog still hovered over the roads, waiting for the warmth of the morning sun to burn it off. She walked the quiet streets, a light mist brushed her skin. A breeze ruffled her dark bangs into her eyes. Jenna swiped them to the side, making a mental note to make an appointment to get them trimmed.

She was surprised when Melissa called her at five this morning and asked her to meet at the park so early. Her best friend rarely woke up before eight, so when she wanted to meet at six-thirty, Jenna jumped out of bed to get ready.

Jenna couldn't imagine what Melissa needed to talk about in person so early in the morning unless something happened with Jake. But why not come to her house? It made no sense. She bit her thumbnail, making up all sorts of issues in her mind as she passed by Susu's Petals, a cute boutique owned by Melissa's soon-to-be sister-in-law.

Susan and her daughter, Megan, walked out of the shop as she passed by. "Morning, Jenna!"

Jenna stopped her progression and turned around to greet Susan. She dropped her concerned frown for Melissa, and she put on the bright expression she showed everyone and chirped, "Good morning!"

Megan ran up to Jenna and thrust open a bright purple umbrella shaped like a cute octopus, "Morning, Miss Jenna! Look at what I have."

"Wow! That's a super cool umbrella. I may need to get one."

Megan grabbed Jenna's hand and started tugging her back to the boutique. "You can. Momma sells them. They also have a big sunshine one. You need that one. It makes me think of you because it has a big smile on it just like you do."

Susan pulled her daughter back gently. "Jenna is going somewhere, Megs. She can come to the boutique later."

Megan pouted. "But I wanted her to see the umbrella."

Jenna squatted down and hugged Megan. "Aww, you are too sweet. I promise I will come back when I get a chance. When you get out of school, you can help me find it."

Megan cheered quickly, appeased, and started playing with her umbrella, opening and closing it.

Jenna stood back up and turned to Susan. "What are you guys doing out here so early?" She looked at her watch. It was almost six-thirty. "School doesn't start for another hour."

Susan answered, buttoning Megan's coat, "Jake asked us to meet him for breakfast at Main Street Java this morning. He wanted to talk to me and Megan about something important."

"Ooh, well, that is something," Jenna turned to Megan, thinking how strange it was that Melissa and her fiancé, Susan's brother, would both want to meet with them separately at the same time. "If it's good news, I hope you let me in on it."

Megan had the tip of the umbrella on the ground and was skipping around it. "Yeppers, I will." She stopped spinning and grabbed her mother's hand. "Come on, Momma. I see Lissy and Uncle Jake."

Jenna and Susan turned to where Megan was pointing. Jake kissed Melissa in front of Main Street Java before he went in, and Melissa started walking down the street to meet them. Susan let her daughter pull her away, laughing, and said over her shoulder, "See you later!"

Jenna smiled and waved. Melissa jogged the rest of the way to meet Jenna. She was smiling. So, Jenna's concerns were for nothing. Her curiosity was bursting now to figure out why Melissa called her so early.

Breathless, Melissa reached her. "Morning! Thanks for waking up so early to meet me."

They crossed the street and headed to the little park snuggled between two buildings. The park used to be an upholstery shop, but it burned down in the seventies. It had remained vacant for years until she and Mel were in seventh grade and the mayor back then had the whole town raise money to turn it into a park.

The two women sat on the park bench. Melissa pulled Snickerdoodle, her tiny Yorkie, out of her tote. The dog was dressed in a yellow raincoat and boots. Jenna laughed. "Oh my gosh, that has to be the most adorable outfit yet."

Melissa shifted Snickerdoodle to one hand, pulled out her phone, and handed it to Jenna. "Let's take a picture."

"What is that smile about?"

Mel held the dog up between the two girls' faces, and Jenna snapped the picture and handed Melissa back her phone. Melissa opened the image. "We all are wearing yellow. If you had blonde hair instead of dark brown, we would all look related."

"Well," Jenna pointed to a little of Snickerdoodle's fur poking out of the hat. "We still could be, see. Her fur right here is starting to get a little darker."

Both women chuckled, and Melissa rubbed her puppy's head. Then, she hooked the leash on Snickerdoodle's collar and set her on the ground to roam about. "I think her big girl fur is going to be a little darker. Can you believe she is almost five months old?"

3

"Time flies."

"It sure does. Actually, that is one of the reasons I called so early. I was too excited to wait."

Jenna couldn't help but feel the excitement bouncing off Melissa and started to practically bounce in her seat. "What the heck is going on? I was so worried for a moment when you called so early. You never wake up before eight or nine. So, spill, I'm dying here."

Melissa squealed. "Jake and I set a date!"

Jenna grinned. "Finally, but why couldn't that wait?"

"Well, we just set it this morning. We stayed up all night talking. I haven't slept yet."

Jenna scooted closer to Melissa and hugged her. "I am so happy for you." When she sat back, she asked, "So when is the date?"

"June fourth."

Jenna looked at her fingers and counted. "Mel! That is only three months away."

"I know, but we don't want to wait anymore, and we started looking at houses online. We have a few appointments set up with the bank and a realtor. Jake's telling Susan and Megan now, but I wanted to talk to you alone because I have a huge favor to ask."

Jenna watched as Melissa's excitement turned to nerves as she got up, wiped her palms on her jeans, and brought Snickerdoodle back to the bench. Jenna grabbed Mel's free hand. "Honey, you don't have to be worried; you're my best friend. I will do anything for you."

Melissa buried her face behind Snickerdoodle. "I'm not sure you're going to like this favor."

"Spit it out. You're making me nervous now."

"We'll it's really two favors. First, will you be my maid of honor?"

Jenna laughed. "Of course, I'd be honored! And what's the second favor?"

"I want you to design and make my wedding dress."

Jenna felt the color drain from her face. Since Christmas, Melissa was the only person in town who knew that Jenna inherited her uncle's skills at fashion design. Technically Jenna's family also knew she could sew, but she never told anyone that she had been making all of her own dresses and gowns for a while now. Melissa found out that the black dress she wore on her first date with Jake and the '50s-inspired dress she wore when the mayor married her dad last Christmas was Jenna's design. After that, Melissa kept insisting Jenna convert her shop into a store to sell her own clothes, but that idea was not something she could consider. Maybe in the past, but not now. Too many things changed.

Snickerdoodle's bark broke Jenna's train of thought. Melissa loosened her grip on her puppy. "Well? Will you? I mean, all the dresses you've made me and never told me or anyone were all amazing. I always thought your uncle sent them, but now that I know it was you, I can't think of any more memorable or special gift you could give me for my wedding. I think my mom would have been so proud of you."

Jenna wanted to cry. Melissa's mom had been like a second mom to her growing up, and she always used to buy her fabric scraps so Jenna could make barbie doll clothes. Melissa's mom even had a sewing machine in the spare room for when they wanted to play design shop. So, the thought of Mel's mom not being there for her wedding, and the fact she probably would be proud made up Jenna's mind for her.

"Okay, I'll do it, but you have to swear to me that you won't tell a single soul besides Jake, of course, that I am making this dress. I can't have it out in the open. I'm not ready for that."

Melissa rushed to hug Jenna. "Thank you, you're the absolute best. I promise.

CHAPTER TWO

*J*enna closed her shop for a few days while she frantically drew designs and pulled fabrics, cutting silks and pinning pieces to a body form, trying to get ideas. With the date of the wedding so near, that didn't give Jenna much time to figure things out, and she had texted her Uncle Max to FaceTime her the moment he had some free time. Preferably before her lunch date with Melissa to discuss some final options.

After she had been working for nearly four hours straight, she texted him again, pleading with him to call her so he could help her figure out how to make the slip she'd pinned on the body form into what she drew. Finally, the phone rang.

She answered the phone without any greeting, instead, she cried out into the screen at her uncle's aged face. "This is a disaster!"

Through the video chat, her uncle Max furrowed his brow.

"Jenna, darling, turn the screen around and bring me closer to the dress."

"Max, there's no sense in showing you. It's not like you can fix it from New York over the phone."

"Darling, stop with the dramatics. That is my department. Now flip that phone around and let me have a look."

Jenna flipped the phone around and walked over to the beginnings of what would become a champagne-colored silk wedding gown. It was pinned to a body form crammed into the corner of her small sewing room in her monogram shop.

"Jenna, this is only the lining. I am sure whatever you design will look exquisite on Melissa. Now tell me what has you in tears."

She spun the phone around. "I'm not cut out for this. This dress is the first dress that I am making that will be on display and to make it more stressful, it's for my best friend's wedding."

"And?" Max drew the word out.

Jenna plopped down on a tiny hot pink futon sofa across from her sewing machine and puffed. "And, I just found out Blair will be at the wedding."

Then after a few seconds of watching Jenna pout through the phone, he said, "Am I supposed to know who Blair is?"

"She's the girl who was all over social media last Christmas. Remember? I sent you the wedding of Melissa's dad that she live-streamed over YouTube."

Max's brows shot up and he whistled through his teeth. "Ah, yes, that video had over a hundred thousand views if I recall."

"Yep. Melissa, being Melissa, became friends with Blair strangely after she told her ex, Paul, that Blair was interested in him. Once they started dating, Blair started calling Mel for advice. Their entire friendship is weird, but now she is coming to the wedding. She will be judging me as the maid of honor and Mel's best friend and posting everything we do online. That alone is horrifying. I love seeing everyone, but I don't want to be in the spotlight. I don't want to be all over social media. It freaks me out knowing that someone out there might recognize me and come track me down."

"Honey, don't you think that you're being a little paranoid? I don't think a little social media here and there will bring stalkers to your door. You lived in the city with me for a couple of years and weren't this afraid. What's this really about?"

Jenna slumped in her seat and bit her thumbnail.

"Stop that."

Jenna removed her nail from her mouth and gripped the phone with both hands. She rested her elbows on her knees, face close to the screen. She spoke softly as if about to tell Max a secret. "Okay, I'll spill. I'm worried once Blair sees the dress, she'll want to know all about the designer. When she finds out this, *nobody*—" Jenna sat up and pointed to herself "—from Cypressville designed it, the wedding will be roasted all over the internet. So, I will humiliate Melissa in front of all of Blair's social media following."

Max huffed over the phone.

"Don't roll your eyes, Max. I'm serious. Since Melissa planned the best Christmas festival our town has ever seen, social media took to it like flies to honey. I mean, I'm grateful and all because our economy skyrocketed, and the traffic of visitors coming in and out has been incredible. But I'm freaking out. What if—" Jenna cut herself off. She watched her own eyes widen in the small box in the upper right corner of the phone screen as she almost told Max her secret. Wanting to hide the expression, she turned her head, looking at the body form holding the pinned-up slip. She continued in the same hushed tones.

"What if whoever is watching and following Blair's vlogs only sees me as Jenna, the town blabbermouth, and tote bag monogram girl, a nobody, trying to play designer. This is too important. I don't want to be a laughingstock and ruin Melissa's wedding or her new business."

Max took a deep breath. Jenna turned to watch him, and her stomach twisted in knots as he stared silently and intensely at her through the phone, trying to read her. Her eyes started to burn, the rims filled with tears. She had a feeling he knew—

Max tutted and finally spoke. "What does Melissa say to all of this nonsense you're spouting?"

Jenna took a deep breath, relieved, then turned away from the phone, blinking her eyes a few times to stop the tears from falling and keep herself from spilling her guts even further. Her shoulders slumped slightly in relief, but then she sat up straight and told Max what he needed to hear. "Melissa is a sweetheart. She'd never be honest."

Exasperated, Max asked, "Darling, what did she say?"

Grudgingly Jenna answered with half-truths. She hadn't told Melissa anything. "She always thinks I'm being silly, but Max, Melissa practically wears a capsule wardrobe all the time. She doesn't know better, the only stylish clothes she wears are the things you send me that don't quite fit right, or I give to her."

"I think Melissa is one smart woman giving you this chance. One thing I did see in that Christmas video was the beautiful dress she wore at the wedding. Who designed that?" he asked with a smirk and a raised brow.

"Hush, Max. She thought you sent that to her until you acted surprised about how well it turned out and fit her perfectly. In fact, my being in this predicament is your fault. She fussed at me for almost two weeks that I had hidden this talent from her and lied about all the dresses I made her."

Max laughed heartily. "My girl, you certainly are an enigma. I'm glad Melissa found out. It's about time someone else sees your ability for what it is, pure genius."

Jenna felt her cheeks redden at her uncle's compliment.

"Honestly, I am surprised she hadn't figured it out earlier. I mean, you've been making things for yourself and drawing countless designs and patterns since you were both children. You even made all of your Barbie doll clothes. She had to know you were under my wing here in the city after high school. I find it hard to believe you've kept your talents hidden from your family and dear friends. Child, I know it's in your blood, you are my niece, after all, and I know you love it because, for the past eight years, you've tried to send me designs under fake names."

Jenna interrupted, shocked. "I nev—"

"Don't deny it, child." He held up his hand to the screen. Jenna bit her tongue as he carried on. "I'd know your designs anywhere. Just because you tried to be sneaky doesn't hide the fact that even you know deep inside, you have a gift. It disappoints me that you still have such low confidence."

Jenna wanted to argue it wasn't all low confidence but fear of being discovered and having her face plastered everywhere. She screwed up years ago and was afraid of being found and having to fess up to her past childishness that had brought her back home to pick up the pieces. Not even Max knew the real reason for her fears.

"Darling, I have been telling you that you are a diamond in the rough for years. It's time to believe in yourself and shine."

Jenna groaned.

Max ignored her. "Text me the design for the dress."

Without a word, she swiped the chat app up to go to her photo album app. Finding the design, she texted it to her uncle then reopened the chat app. "I just sent it."

Max's phone dinged. His face disappeared, leaving a black screen with pause typed in the center. Jenna bit her thumbnail, brow scrunched in worry as her uncle reviewed her design.

His face came back into view a minute later, expressionless. "Your design is classic with a twist of whimsy. Seductive, yet innocent. Very unique."

Jenna's stomach twisted into knots. "What does that even mean?"

"Darling, stop your worries. That was a compliment. This design is something many women today would want, I assure you. I could easily see your designs paired with the tuxes I design."

Jenna sank back into her seat, relieved that he didn't rip her design apart like he did when she worked with him back in New York.

"You have to say nice things to me because you trained me years ago." She glanced at the dress hanging on the body form, disappointed. "I sadly know the truth."

Max rolled his eyes again. "Child, this is ridiculous."

He walked over to his window, his video shaking with each step. Jenna could hear the traffic through the phone. He sighed. "It's been a very long time since I've been home. Things here are practically running themselves with all of my assistants. Would it make you feel better if I came down there for support?"

Jenna stared at the phone for several seconds in shock. Then, finally, she sat up straighter and started to bounce in her seat. "Oh my gosh, you are brilliant. Yes, please come into town. That way, whenever Blair comes, she can meet you, and you can pretend to be the designer. I mean, you are well known all over the world. Melissa's wedding will go down in history as another win, and you will bring in more tourists just by being here if Blair posts about you."

She took a deep breath and rushed out, "Please, Uncle Max." Jenna batted her eyes and gave her uncle her best puppy dog face. "I won't feel so stressed if you're here, and the attention won't be on me anymore. You know how I am. And I know with you here this dress will end up magazine-worthy."

Max made a noncommittal noise as he stroked his fingers in his long white beard, which had started trending on social media this past year. Since growing it, he'd been noted in some articles as the classy Saint Nick of fashion. Uncle Max, also known as Maximilian Thorne, was one of the top designers in men's fashion and had recently taken to modeling his creations. His suits and tuxedos were worn by more stars than Jenna could count, and sometimes while talking to her uncle, she forgot he was famous. Funny how when she lived in New York, she tried to hide the fact she knew him, and now she wanted to exploit him.

Thinking back on his offer to come to Cypressville she wondered what gave him a change of heart. She couldn't remember a time when he'd come home. In the past, he point-blank refused and would instead send money for her and her family to visit him in New York.

"Well? Will you come?"

"Darling, I don't think it's a good idea for me to take credit for your designs. You worked hard on them. It's time to own them. Plus, if they hit social media as if I designed them, I will have women pestering me to design their gowns, and you know I don't swing that way. I much prefer the male clientele."

Was that a no? Was it an impulse offer? Is this his way of getting out of coming? "Please, I need you, Max. I never asked for anything, even when I followed you around as your assistant for years. I learned everything you threw at me, did everything you asked, but I'm asking now. Will you please come and save me?"

"Didn't I save you once before when you cried for weeks on end over here and decided you wanted to go home? And once home, your parents had to call me after you arrived because you were in a depressed state for months. Not much I could do from over here, but if I recall, I had to practically pressure you into some sort of career, and I even bought you the building for your monogram shop."

"Ugh, alright, you don't have to rub that in my face."

"I'm not trying to rub anything in your face. I'm not exactly sure what happened back then, and I am not going to ask because I know that whoever hurt you made you miserable, and I know that feeling very well."

Jenna looked at her uncle over the phone. "How did you know I was having a hard time with a breakup?"

Max had an age-old sad look in his eyes. "Because I see that look in my eyes when I think of going back to Cypressville."

Jenna gasped. "Is that why you never come home? Tell me

who hurt you, and I will tell you if they are still here. Maybe you've been staying away for nothing and —"

"No, he is still there, and I am the one who hurt him. I've seen him on Instagram. I followed the group of influencers who were there at Christmas."

"Max, I'm so sorry. You don't have to come home. I will manage."

"I know you will manage because I taught you everything you know, and you have the innate skill and a sharp eye. But I think maybe it's time I leave the past in the past and come home. I've been missing my roots as I age, and at seventy, I feel like it's time to reconcile my loose ends."

A moment of fear traveled through Jenna. Even though she called Max her uncle, he was more like her grandpa. He is her dad's uncle and basically raised her dad when his father died. "Loose ends, what do you mean? Are you sick?"

Max laughed. "Goodness no! I just meant that as you age, you start ruminating on your past and the what-ifs. I could have done things differently. Times were different in small Southern towns, and I wasn't ready to fight the fight. I think it's time I made amends."

Jenna melted into her sofa. Then, finally, she brought the phone back up to her face. "Thank goodness you are well, but now I'm curious. Who's the mystery man that stole your heart?"

He gave Jenna a mischievous smirk and his eyes twinkled as he brought his phone closer to his face, as if he were about to tell her. "That's for me to know and you to find out."

A door opening and the chatter of people could be heard coming from the background on Max's end of the call. He turned his head and said something to someone. "Sorry, darling, I need to go. I'll text you when I can make it into town. I'm hoping to tie up a few projects by the weekend. Then I believe I will be onwards to Cypressville."

He took a deep breath, closed his eyes for a moment. When he opened them again to the noise in his office increasing, he hurriedly blew Jenna a few kisses, and she returned them as she pressed "end." She threw the phone on the sofa cushion beside her. She slumped into the seat and grabbed a throw pillow, hugging it to her chest as she sighed in relief. Uncle Max would give her the courage and strength to finish Melissa's dress, and she would hopefully let everyone except Melissa and Jake believe he was the designer.

CHAPTER THREE

*B*en walked through the garage door, entering the kitchen of the two-story, Colonial-style home in Metairie, Louisiana, where he grew up. His mom swayed to a soft classic rock song while scooping up the fresh-cut fruit and transferring it to a bowl. She hadn't heard him enter.

A wicked grin spread across his lips as he snuck up behind her, and put his hands on her shoulders. Startled, she yelped and squirmed away from him as she threw a handful of fruit in the air.

"Benjamin James Sanderson, you gave me a fright!"

He laughed as he picked up a pineapple chunk from the counter and popped it into his mouth. "Morning, Umma."

His mom picked up a towel and wiped her hands, then wound it and swatted him, aiming at his thigh. He scooted back, but the snap of the tip still got him.

He rubbed the sting out. "Dang Umma, that smarts."

"It should. It's not like I didn't do it enough to you growing up. Always making mischief, trying to overstep the line." She handed him the towel.

"Now help me clean up the mess before your father comes in.

With what you are going to approach him with this morning, we don't need to put him in a mood."

Ben's father loved order. As a disabled Marine sergeant, he ran his house and business in perfect order. When he lost his leg during the Gulf War, he had to learn to build his life up again and create a new routine. Then eight years ago, he had a massive heart attack and felt like his body let him down. The military paid for therapy for the entire family. The new adjustment had been hard for them all.

Since then, Ben's dad never wanted to travel anymore, made Ben work like a dog, and none of them ever got to go back to Korea to visit his grandparents and extended family. Ben missed it, he knew his mom did too, but she never complained. That was one of the reasons he worked so hard. He wanted to make sure that he and his dad made enough money to always have his grandparents flown in twice a year. But lately, his grandparents didn't want to travel either. It was like everything was changing, urging him to get his dad to change too.

It was time.

Ben started to pick up the fallen fruit from the floor and place it in the garbage disposal. He often thought about what direction his life would have taken if his dad had never had a heart attack and if he hadn't left his last semester at NYU to move home and help out. After a year of his dad's recovery, Ben moved back to Manhattan, got a job, and searched all his old haunts for the strange girl he met his last semester there who wouldn't give him her last name or address. But after six months, his dad fell ill again, and he had to move back home.

She was beautiful, intelligent, and creative, and Ben still dreamed about her. Besides her lack of personal information, they had so many things in common. None of the other women that he dated made him feel the way he had when they were together.

Ben sighed, trying to shake her from his thoughts. He couldn't understand why it got harder and harder each year rather than easier. Didn't time heal all wounds? Obviously not. His dad was a prime example of a man who struggled to heal from change.

This time of year always was more difficult for his entire family. It reminded them all of when life changed, but it reminded Ben mostly of his greatest regret. It was a beautiful, sunny spring morning when Ben met her in Central Park for coffee before class. She had been on a blanket leaning back on her hands, her head tilted toward the sun, her long black hair touching the ground. He had bent over her, casting a shadow over her face, and she opened one of her light green eyes at him. A grin and a giggle escaped her lips.

He leaned down to kiss her, and as they broke apart, he handed her the caramel mocha he had brought. She was the first person he'd met who loved coffee as much as he did.

That night he had big plans. Ben had invited her to dinner at her favorite restaurant. He hoped by expressing his love, he'd convince her to trust him with her last name and finally give him her phone number since he'd be going back home for the summer. They had been meeting up every morning at the coffee house for four months, planning each date before leaving the last one. He'd been patient playing by her rules, but that night he was ready to pull the information out of her.

Hours after they made plans, he got the call. His dad had a heart attack, and he hurriedly packed up to leave. He never made it back to New York. His roommate had to pack the rest of his belongings and ship them to him.

She was in his past. He'd never see her again. His therapist told him the reason he still thought about her so often was that he genuinely cared for the girl, and he carried guilt for leaving without a trace, along with regrets for respecting her wishes in playing along with her game and not getting her phone number.

His mom knocked his shoulder with hers. "Ben, hun, it will be alright. Dad's moods have been better lately. I honestly think this may be good for him. You need a break, and he needs to learn by working full-time for a while that it's time for him to retire and for us to travel. I'll have your back."

Ben hugged his mom. "Love you," he whispered into her perfectly coiffed hair. "Umma, don't you worry about me. I'm willing to put up with Dad's mood. Dr. Ledinsky was at the office with Dad after golf, and I overheard him tell Dad again it's time for him to let the reins go and retire. I am finally at the point where I won't continue working with him." After almost losing one of his best editors, who also happened to be his best friend, he had a wake-up call. Dad fumed for weeks after Ben overrode his acceptance of Jake Blessing's resignation, but keeping Jake working remotely had given him the most amazing plans for the future of Sanderson Press. It could save them this fiscal quarter. "Actually––"

"Benjamin."

Ben stiffened at his dad's voice coming from behind him. He turned around. Ben's father, Jonathan Sanderson, stood in the entryway from the dining area to the kitchen, arms crossed, eyes cold and squinting, and all burly six-foot-four, intimidating as hell. The fact that he couldn't look down on Ben any longer took away the fear his dad used to inflict on him as a kid, but not the look of disappointment that always seemed to linger behind his dad's eyes these past few months.

Ben's heart clenched, and his stomach soured, but he hid the sadness that disappointment caused him. Instead, he mimicked his dad's stance. "Morning, Dad."

"Son." His dad nodded then looked beyond him, giving his wife one of his pointed stares. "Joon."

Joon passed by them with the bowl of fruit. As she passed her husband, Ben heard her whisper, "Be nice." She led the way into the dining area. "Boys, let's eat breakfast. You can talk over the meal."

Joon puckered her lips and knocked her husband on the arm

with her elbow, making smooching sounds until Jonathan visibly relaxed. Ben's dad bent down so his wife could kiss his cheek and a soft smile crept onto his lips. Ben's parents didn't lack love, and his mom could always ease the tension from his dad's face.

Within seconds the entire energy in the room changed. Ben relaxed.

"Your umma's right. Let's talk over breakfast."

Ben and his dad grabbed a plate as his mom returned to the kitchen to grab the coffee carafe and the orange juice.

After they all started eating, Jonathan broke the silence. "What is it that you wanted to talk about?"

"Dad, I overheard Dr. Ledinsky and you talking the other day."

His dad served himself some eggs and bacon. "I'm not retiring if that's what you're aiming at."

Ben looked at his mom sitting across from him, serving herself. She made a slight nod.

"I wanted to talk to you about the next fiscal quarter."

His dad's right brow shot up. He put his fork down and turned toward Ben. "What about it?"

"Dad, you can't deny the numbers of the last two quarters. Sanderson Press needs to make some changes if we are to stay open. More and more new authors are self-publishing and working with the new print-on-demand machine to print their books. When we had to retire our old, outdated printing press years ago…." He trailed off, assessing his dad's reactions. Jonathan was still sensitive over the fact that his health and medical bills interfered with his ability to maintain the bindery. Ben had always felt guilty that he couldn't keep it running properly and felt his father blamed him for its disrepair. His dad scowled. When he didn't comment, Ben continued, "We took a huge financial hit when we shut down our bindery and began outsourcing."

Jonathan grunted and nodded. Ben, slightly encouraged,

continued. "When Jake went remote, it gave me an idea how to cut costs without compromising the quality of customer service you founded this company on and bring back the press."

Jonathan hadn't moved, but he lifted his brows slightly. Ben had his attention. His dad had hated having to stop printing when the machine cost more to repair than print. Ben took a deep breath.

"I talked to a realtor a few days ago."

Jonathan shifted and crossed his arms over his chest. "And, why would you need a realtor? Are you selling your house?"

"Well, not quite. I got them to look at our building."

His dad slammed his hand on the table. "No! Absolutely not!"

"Dad, we're using less than half the space. It takes up more than half of our income to pay the costs to keep it up and running. If we sell, we can get a smaller space and have our employees work remotely. We could implement savings and utilize independent contractors as we grow and the need arises. It's something to consider."

"No! Absolutely not."

"Then I'm done. I can't work like this anymore. I'm exhausted trying to keep us above water. You have to see that Sanderson Press will soon be bankrupt if we don't do something to make changes."

"Benjamin, the subject is closed. You are the CEO and will not abandon your station."

"Dad!" Ben practically shouted.

His dad sat erect in his chair, glaring at him.

Joon quickly stood up and walked behind Ben's dad, placing her hands on his shoulders. She leaned down and gave her husband a quick kiss on his cheek. His mom knew his dad's love language well.

While she gently massaged Jonathan's shoulders, she changed the topic. "Benjamin, isn't Jake getting married soon?"

Instant relief engulfed the room. "Yes, in a few months."

His mom turned to his dad. "Jonathan, why don't you give Benny the next three months off until after Jake's wedding. That way, he can have a much-needed vacation, and you can see to the company. Then, talk to James in accounting and have him show you the books and think about what Ben has told you. It will be good for you both."

His dad was about to remark, but his mom placed her finger over Jonathan's lips. "You've taken Benny for granted lately. He's been walking in your shadow long enough. It's time you go back to work full-time instead of just sitting in your office to get out of the house. Maybe working full days for three months will remind you of why I am ready for you to retire."

Ben turned to his mom, gave her a crooked smile, and hope filled his eyes. She was an angel. Even though she rarely questioned her husband's ideals or interfered in business, she did have a way of making his dad listen to her. Ben waited patiently for his dad to process her words and respond.

"Your mother may have a point. She has been getting on to me about retiring for a while now." Jonathan glanced at Joon then Ben. The air seemed to let out of his body, relaxing his stern posture for only a moment before he sat straight once more. For the first time in years, Ben saw resignation in his dad's eye. Jonathan sighed, concentrated on eating a bite of fruit, and after a few seconds he said, "You haven't had a day off in practically eight years. I shouldn't have neglected to offer you time off. Every good man needs a break, and you are a good man, Ben. Take the three months off, and after your friend is married, we can revisit this discussion."

Ben opened and closed his mouth a few times, not knowing what to say. He honestly wasn't expecting the time off or that his dad would possibly agree. He was still upset that Ben renegotiated Jake's resignation and offered him more money and a contract position to keep him at the company because he was his friend. But it wasn't all nepotism. Jake was the best editor in the

South East Region and he'd be a fool to lose him without a fight. Ben had truly mentally prepared for more arguments and was grateful it went so well. The rest of breakfast was less tense and almost enjoyable with his umma's change of topic to Jake's wedding.

W hen Ben opened the doors to the large building that housed Sanderson Press, the excitement started to sink in that he was finally able to get away for a holiday. Jenna crept into his mind. He wished she would leave him alone, but that woman and all of his regrets about how he left would haunt him for the rest of his life. Maybe a vacation and spending three months in Cypressville with Jake would get her out of his mind.

CHAPTER FOUR

*T*he morning dragged on after hanging up with Max. Jenna had about three hours to waste before meeting Melissa for lunch to go over the final design for the dress. She had been procrastinating showing the design to her, but the wedding was only three months away now, and Melissa was getting anxious.

Jenna skimmed the designs on her tablet and her stomach churned as she stared at each one, imagining the dress falling apart as Melissa walked down the aisle. She threw the tablet down on the sofa, and rested her head in her hands, rubbing her scalp and taking deep breaths.

The chime in her shop rang, and she heard a man's voice call out, "Hello!"

Jenna's head popped up so fast at the sound of that voice. It was eerily familiar. The stress was finally getting to her. It couldn't be who she thought it was, that would be impossible.

Jenna walked out of her sewing room into the small break room where last Christmas she had the nerve to tell Melissa that her and Jake's relationship was too much trouble and that love should be easy. Melissa didn't know about Jenna's fling in

Manhattan. That the man she met there had ruined her and prevented her from ever finding love again. If Melissa had known, she wouldn't have answered with the words that still rang in Jenna's ears, "Where is your love, Jenna?"

"Trapped in the past." Jenna had thought that day.

Not one relationship since then had felt easy. But that relationship in New York had been doomed, and it was all her fault. If she weren't so insecure and hiding that she was a world-famous clothing designer's niece, she wouldn't have wasted nearly four months stringing Ben along. The first time they met, Ben practically knocked her off her feet. His expression of pure horror and embarrassment made the initial frustration of being knocked over go away. She couldn't help as laughter escaped her lips. The way he looked at her like a forlorn puppy when she got on the bus made her smile, though he was quite endearing in his mannerisms compared to the well-put-together attire he wore.

Then the next morning when they ended up at the same coffee shop, they ordered the same thing at the same time by different cashiers, and hadn't realized they were beside one another until the barista called out, "Caramel mocha latte!" Ben knocked into her as they both turned to grab for it. The first thing she noticed was a smooth hand with long fingers created for the piano and a cufflink designed by her uncle. When she looked up, it was the man who had knocked her over at the bus stop.

"You again! What are the odds?" she said as she let him have the coffee.

He smiled and with a slight chuckle and gave her the coffee. "I'll wait. It's the least I can do after making a fool out of myself yesterday."

They ended up at the coffee shop at the same time each morning for a few days, not once exchanging their names, even though they sat together drinking and talking. He was reserved yet had a charming quirk about him that made her want to spend more time with him. Only she was worried that since he was obviously into fashion that he might be like all the other guys she dated and try to take advantage of her relationship with her famous uncle, Max. Their fourth date was when she had the idea to play a game of chance, and when she created the rules for the game.

She called it serendipity, based on a movie she once saw — if they were meant to be, they'd meet up again by chance somewhere in the city. Of course, she was crushing on him, so they still made dates, but she stuck to her rules: no last names, no phone numbers, no family names or histories until they met randomly five times outside of their planned dates. They had to follow the rules no matter how long it took for those five meetings, even if they decided they were falling for each other. Only after the five serendipitous meetings could they make it official because, by that time, they would be bound to have fallen in love.

That day happened.

They made their last date where she was going to tell him she was in love with him, but he no-showed. She couldn't believe that after all those months and chance meetings he stood her up. Her heart was broken. She shook the thought from her mind and tidied her mussed-up hair in the mirror by the door to the shop. Walking through the door, she called out, "Hello?" as the bell on the door chimed, and all she saw was the back of a tall, well-dressed, slender man with dark hair leaving the shop.

Jenna shivered as goosebumps rose on her arms with a sense of déjà vu lurking in her mind. "Strange," she muttered, rubbing her arms as she turned around to go back and start cutting fabric.

CHAPTER FIVE

The weather was perfect outside and Jenna wished she would have told Melissa she'd meet her at the park instead of Main Street Java. The trees lining the street were all green and the shade of them kept the start of the Southern heat in the mid-seventies. Jenna rushed past her friend Susan's shop and waved through the window as she headed to the cafe. Nearly every available space was now rented and doing well since the influencers were hired last Christmas.

Jenna waved and said hello to several passersby as she speed-walked to her lunch with Melissa. She was nearly twenty minutes late and the phone ringing had brought her out of a work trance. She had finally shaken off the déjà vu after the strange man came and went and got to work cutting out the bodice pattern she finally decided on for Melissa's wedding gown. The completed underlining was created to fit any of her designs, so she was glad to have that done and out of the way. There were only three months left for her to finish but knowing Max would soon be here alleviated a ton of pressure.

She sped through the cafe door and waved to Walter, the owner, behind the counter as she skidded to a stop at Mel's table.

Out of breath, Jenna plopped into the chair and took a sip of the glass of water Melissa had waiting on her side of the table.

"I took the privilege of ordering," Melissa said. "I was too hungry to wait."

Snickerdoodle, was in her hands, lapping up her puppuccino. Jenna reached over to pet her head. "I'm so sorry, I was caught up in cutting out the pattern for your gown."

"Well, in that case, you are totally forgiven, huh, Snickerdoodle?"

Snickerdoodle looked up at Melissa as if she completely understood and barked one quick little sound.

Jenna laughed. "Thanks. What's for lunch?"

"Ham and cheese croissants."

"I should have known. That's what you always get."

"Yep. So, can you show me which design you ended up choosing?"

"Of course, it's your gown. You need to know what you'll be wearing." Jenna pulled the tablet out of her purse and handed it over to Melissa.

Melissa held Snickerdoodle out to Jenna and they made a swap.

Jenna now understood why Melissa loved the dog so much. Over the last month, anytime Jenna showed Mel some of her designs, Mel would pass the dog over to her. When she did, Jenna would bury her face in Snickerdoodle's fur near her neck. The little dog would rub up against her or lick her nose or cheek, and it would instantly give her a sense of calm. It helped her so much that she had started to consider adopting and went to the shelter. But she just wasn't quite ready for the dedication that came with caring for a pet, especially when she had so much on her plate getting this gown ready in less than three months.

Jenna couldn't take the silence anymore. "Well?"

"Jenna, I swear this is probably the most beautiful gown I've ever seen. Why in the world have you been hiding your talent behind your monogramming machine and fibbing to me and the world about what you are capable of. I'm a little hurt that you never told me I was wearing your creation this past Christmas until I overheard Max and you talking about it."

Jenna breathed out deeply, some of the butterflies leaving with the exhale. All she did was lift her shoulders up and down, not knowing how to explain her fears. Jenna knew that she had talent. It was her fear of becoming Max, a person who was sought-after, who appeared in magazines. That someone might find her and come back, and she would have to pick up the broken pieces of her heart and fake not being hurt by his utter and complete rejection of her.

"I am going to let people believe Max designed your gown," she told Melissa, "so please don't tell anyone it was me. Just tell anyone who asked that I helped in creating it, and that's all."

Melissa put the tablet on the table and stared at Jenna, who buried her face in Snickerdoodle's fur.

"I swear, Jenna, with talent like yours, I don't understand why you are so incredibly afraid. I mean, I'll keep your secret because I'm your best friend and all, but I still don't get it. You really need to get over this fear of being compared to Max or whatever it is that's really preventing you from selling your designs."

"Um, if I remember correctly, you quit being an event planner because you were afraid of your name being dragged through the mud and hid the fact you saved Christmas. The least you can do is support me like I did you by keeping things hush-hush."

Melissa blushed. Jenna knew she couldn't counter that because Melissa knew it was true. She grumbled as she reached over the table for her dog. "Stop hiding behind my Snickky."

"Snickky?" Jenna laughed, relieved that Melissa would allow the topic to be dropped. "When did she get that nickname?"

Melissa's frown turned into a giggle. "Jake was taking her outside to do her business. I swear he is so funny when he talks to her and doesn't realize I'm around. Anyway, when they were taking too long, I ventured out to meet them, and there he was, practically laying on the grass with her in front of him. He was trying to teach her to roll over, and when she was almost getting it, he said, 'Come on, Snickky, you can do it,' and lo and behold, she took to the nickname, barked, and rolled over."

Jenna tried to cover up her smirk. "Y'all are so stinkin' cute."

"Oh, hush, wait until you meet someone. I'm sure you will be even stinkier in your cuteness because of your bubble gum personality."

"Hey, that's not nice," Jenna pouted but struggled to keep it up when Melissa stuck her tongue out behind Snickerdoodle like a little kid herself.

They both started laughing, and Melissa said, "See! Nothing upsets you."

Jenna felt like a bucket of cold water dropped over her. "That's not true." Just that morning, she was thinking of the one thing in her life that had devastated her, the one thing she couldn't forgive herself for, the one thing that upset her and sent her into a deep depression for half a year.

"There are a ton of things that bother me. I think I'm just better at hiding them than others."

"Well, I've known you since we were practically in diapers, and the only time you ever seemed out of sorts was when you had to move home from New York."

"That's because you were away at college, and I knew how to put on a fake smile when I got to see my BFF for only a few days out of a semester. I didn't want to ruin our time with my moods."

There were times Jenna wished she would have told Melissa the truth, but too many years had passed, and now it was too late. Mel would probably be hurt to know Jenna hadn't confided in her. It still depressed her that she really never got over that experience and that after eight years, Ben still haunted her. Like earlier today, when she could have sworn that was his voice calling out hello. He had said it the same way he always did when he'd greet her. Long and drawn out, reminding her of home. She often wondered where from the South he was from, but that was another of her stupid rules. No background info on one another until they decided to make their relationship official. She had been dead set on making sure whatever guy she dated liked her for her and not her past, or her uncle, or anything. She wanted to be sure their love could be real. Ben hesitated at the rules at first. After a few meetings, finding out that they both had a passion for zombie movies, dystopian books, and a love for every art museum in the city kept him playing her game.

"Here's your lunch, girls." Walter placed their sandwiches, and a treat for Snickerdoodle in front of them, interrupting her thoughts.

"Thanks, Walter," Melissa responded as she placed Snicker-doodle in her tote on the floor and gave her the cookie. She then pulled out some hand sanitizer and squirted some in her hands, then tilted it toward Jenna as if in question.

Jenna put her hand under the bottle and tried to get out of her funk again. She placed a fake smile on her lips and lifted her sandwich. "Thanks." She took a big bite to distract Melissa from hopefully catching on that her spirits were down.

Jenna had to start patting herself on the back for good acting. Melissa smiled back and started chattering away about her wedding. Then her face brightened up even more, and her eyes got wide. "Oh, I've been meaning to tell you Jake's best man got into town almost a week ago without telling us. Jake ran into him roaming around Main Street this morning. He texted me to see if we could plan a meet and greet this weekend to introduce you."

"Oh, I can't."

Melissa's face dropped. "What? Why?"

"Girl, you'll never believe who I'm going to be seeing this weekend." Jenna took a bite of her sandwich.

"Oh my gosh! You're talking to someone and you didn't tell me! How could you?"

Melissa genuinely looked hurt, and Jenna knew once more there was no way she could ever tell her this late in the game that she would probably be single the rest of her life because she knew she'd never find love again.

"Seriously, I hate it when you leave me hanging with a juicy bit of gossip. What is going on this weekend?" Melissa practically whined.

"Uncle Max is coming into town."

Melissa's jaw dropped. "No way!"

"Yes, way!"

"Seriously? Max never comes here. What in the world made him change his mind? He even told me not to waste an invitation on him because no matter how much he loved me and thought of me like family, he wouldn't be coming. Too many bad memories with our little town."

"Well, your wedding, for one, did get him thinking of coming back, but the main thing is he is going to help me with your dress."

Melissa squealed in excitement.

"But I have even juicier gossip." Both girls leaned into the table, and Jenna whispered, "Max was in love with someone here, and he hasn't been able to come back since because of how the town reacted to their relationship. He couldn't handle the stress of everyone staring at him all the time."

Melissa sat back. "How strange. I mean, he's a famous designer, and now a model. People must stare at him all the time."

"True, but back in the eighties, things were different, people were different, bigger cities were more accepting, and he could be himself. I get that. Sometimes it's hard always wearing a mask and pretending life is all rosy."

Jenna sat back. Even though her story and life were very different from her uncle's, she totally understood why he left. Pretending is hard work, and he'd done it for around thirty years and was tired. On the other hand, Jenna had only been pretending for eight, but she was so close to breaking again that she was grateful Max would be back, and that she could take her mind off herself. Maybe he'd teach her how to overcome her fears.

Jenna and Melissa tried to figure out who in town could have been Max's love for the rest of the lunch. They couldn't think of anyone other than Walter, and that was impossible. Walter and Max were complete opposites.

"Why doesn't your dad ever talk about who Max was with? Didn't he live with Max after his parents died?"

"He did from age twelve until Max moved to New York, and he went to college there. Max made my dad promise never to bring up the past to him; he wanted to live in the present. My dad took that to heart. You know him. He never looks back, only looks forward, and he respects Max more than anyone. He'd never betray his trust like that even to me."

"That's why I love your dad. Loyal to the bone, just like you."

Jenna practically wanted to cry at those words. She wasn't loyal. She was a horrible friend. She felt like she betrayed Melissa's trust by not confiding in her all those years ago.

CHAPTER SIX

*B*en had been in town for over a week, enjoying having no responsibilities for the first time in years. He didn't even tell Jake he was in town yet so that he could chill and try and get his mind off of Sanderson Press and what to do about potentially going bankrupt. He procrastinated until the end of the week to let everyone know that he was on temporary leave and that they could talk to his dad. But at the same time, to copy him in all correspondence to keep him in the loop. It was more complicated than he thought to leave and not be checking in every few hours.

Eventually, the assistant he shared with his dad told him not to worry, that she would keep him abreast of anything important, and for him to enjoy his much-needed time off. Cynthia was a gem. They went on a few dates when he moved back from New York but it never worked out, and last year she met her husband, a boy she dated in high school that moved back to New Orleans, Louisiana, and they got married after only three months. Ben and Jake both joked about Tony moving quickly so as to not lose Cynthia a second time.

Ben laughed out loud at that thought. Jake and Melissa sure

beat Tony and Cynthia. It only took him a couple of weeks to propose to Melissa after reconnecting. "I guess if you know, you know," he mumbled out loud, then wondered if he ever saw Jenna again if he'd feel the same connection that they felt back in college. Would he propose to her just as quickly as Jake had to Melissa?

It was odd, Jenna had been on his mind so much that when he came to town, he started thinking he was seeing her everywhere. Yesterday he even walked into a sewing shop, remembering he saw a Jenna lookalike go in there one day. Once he was inside, and no one was at the counter, he quickly turned around and left, berating himself for being foolish even thinking about it.

In the end, he went back to his room at the B and B and called his therapist. Dr. Archer reminded him that he tended to get sentimental about Jenna every year around spring. After all, it was the time of year when he left her, and his dad almost died. She reminded him that the guilt from leaving Jenna without a trace and his frustration with her for playing her game cost him what he believed was his true love. His therapist compared it to grieving someone who died suddenly after a fight or an argument. There was guilt, and things weren't resolved. In a way, he was still mourning her, and all of his stress over his work, which in some ways was similar to the stress he had when his dad was first sick, made him think he saw her all over town. But it was just women who had dark hair or bangs or were around the same height. His being on a vacation of sorts, his mind didn't know how to shut down, and he was thinking of her again.

Ben, still used to his business hours, woke up early. The sweet smell of Camellia trees filled the air as he left the B and B, a historic Victorian home located about two blocks off Marshall Street, to walk over to his favorite place to relax and read the paper in the morning. He stopped into Dorsey's market, which reminded him of some of the small markets back in New York. Mr. Dorsey kept a fresh local fruit and vegetable stand out front, and the inside of the market was small and cramped and smelled of spiced meats they had cooking for plate lunches later in the day. He picked up a couple of different newspapers and headed toward the circle at Marshall and Main to the gazebo in the middle.

The hustle and bustle of Cypressville were slow-paced compared to Uptown New Orleans where his office was located, yet it gave him a strange sense of being home. The early morning shop owners were all friendly and made sure to wave hello, and the tree-lined sidewalks seemed to always have residents or tourists browsing. He had lucked out getting the last room at the B and B when he arrived several weeks ago.

He loved the quiet of the morning, when the street lamps slowly turned off as the sun started to rise. He had about an hour to enjoy his paper and watch the downtown come to life while he waited to meet Jake later for coffee. But this morning he struggled to concentrate on the news. He kept thinking of his therapy session the previous day with Dr. Archer. After all these years, what his therapist had been saying was starting to make sense. His heart still ached for Jenna. The last few times he saw the Jenna lookalikes, he ignored them, knowing his therapist was right. It was probably just his imagination. As if Jenna would look the same as she did nearly eight years ago.

"Ben!" Jake called from Main Street Java with two iced coffees in hand as waited for a car to pass before he crossed the road. Ben waived and stood up as Jake arrived and took the last three steps up to the gazebo. Jake handed a coffee over to Ben.

"Hey man, what's on your agenda today?"

Jake took a sip of his coffee. "Lissy and I are supposed to be meeting up around noon to look at a house. Can you believe it? I'm getting married."

Jake looked happy and baffled at the same time.

"Honestly, man, I think it's insane. I never once heard you talk about Lissy until you came back home last Christmas. All I ever heard you talk about was Molly. The apple of your eye."

"True, that she was." Jake was quiet for a moment. "You know Ben, I never stopped loving Lissy. My heart just grew for Molly, and I think Molly always knew I still held a candle for Lissy. Sometimes I wonder if she wouldn't have passed away in that accident if we had come back here. I sometimes think back on how adamant I was about never coming back home, and if we did, it was only to visit our folks while we were in school, or if I knew for certain Lissy was not home from her college at the time we were going to visit. My sister used to be a doll about keeping me informed back then."

Ben's jaw dropped. "I never in a million years thought I would have heard you say something like that."

Jake rubbed his hand over his heart as if trying to ease the ache. "Honestly, me neither. I loved Molly, I really did, and sometimes I feel guilty knowing that I never loved her nearly as much as I do Lissy. Do you think that is horrible of me?"

They were silent for a while as they drank their coffee. Ben finally responded. "No, I think it's honest. Love comes in many shapes and sizes. Some love is great, and then other times when we love someone it's more magnified. Some say that no matter what happens in your life or who enters it, the dragon deep inside your chest protects it like a secret treasure, not wanting to expose its value so that no one knows of its existence except for the beholder."

Jake laughed a little. "Sounds like someone's taken a liking to fantasy novels lately, but I get your meaning. Thanks for not looking down on me for it."

"I could never look down on love. If anything, I'm a bit jealous. I wish that I could have that kind of love again. I had my chance and lost it years ago."

Jake knocked his shoulder into Ben's gently. "I know that you wish you could find that girl from college again, but I was thinking Lissy's best friend is super sweet. Maybe when y'all meet, you'll hit it off."

"Dude, this is your time, your wedding. I am not looking to date the maid of honor. That just seems wrong on so many levels. This isn't a romance novel. No need to hook me up."

Jake laughed. "That was sappy, wasn't it? It has to be because of the book I'm editing. Janet Gray wrote a wedding romance." Last Christmas Janet nearly fired Sanderson Press as her publishing company because Jake had turned in his resume. Thankfully they worked it all out.

"It takes place in a small town, and I swear there are moments when I think she is basing her characters on us."

"You never know, she very well may be. I mean, if you hadn't told Janet in December you were planning on asking your high school sweetheart to marry you, or gave her the sob story of your misunderstanding, I highly doubt she would have been so keen on allowing us to break her contract with no repercussions to write a new one. This is most likely her payback for the change of terms."

Jake tapped his fingers against his coffee cup. "Have you decided what to do if your dad doesn't want to make the changes to the company?"

The joviality of the moment took a turn, and Ben leaned back on the bench and blew out a breath. "No. Well, sort of."

Ben got up and threw his cup in the trash, and turned to Jake. "You know, man, I've always wanted to own a bookstore. I've invested well into my 401K, and if push came to shove, I could withdraw it for my initial investment, but I'm hoping my dad comes to grips with the reality of our business. But to get him to give up so much and to move toward the future, I need to come up with something more profitable than just selling the building and the old printing press."

"Actually, Lissy and I were talking the other night about how she wished she could find a local place to print books on demand instead of having to order online through the larger manufacturer. Have you ever looked into offering e-book or printing books on demand? I mean, the company started as a book binding company. Maybe it's time to reintroduce it to your clients in a more modern way. Since I've been with the company, we mostly dealt with local authors in and around the tri-state area. Maybe something like this will end up saving you the cost of having to outsource."

Ben started pacing back and forth. "That's what I've been thinking too."

Jake turned to him a bit excitedly. "You know what would be even better is if you opened up a local bookstore like you've always talked about and sold all the books you publish. Maybe give tours to kids in school to learn how the printing of books is done."

Ben's mind raced with all of the possibilities. This might be the answer he'd been looking for. He clapped Jake on the back. "This has to be the best idea I've heard in a week. Why did I never think of something so simple? I knew you were my best friend for a reason. I've gotta run. I have some research to do."

CHAPTER SEVEN

*B*en saw the Jenna lookalike go into Main Street Java, and he nearly choked on his spit while talking on the phone with his Sales Director. He sped up his conversation as his heart thudded in anticipation. It was time to find this woman and put the ghost of Jenna to rest, and finally he had an opportunity. There was no place for her to hide or run anymore. He'd see her close up and prove to himself once and for all that this wasn't Jenna, just his overworked mind wishing for that one piece of calm he had in the past before his life changed forever.

And if no woman existed, he'd be calling Dr. Archer and telling her that he needed a reevaluation.

"Look, Dan, I have to go. Reconfigure the numbers from manufacturing to in-house printing with the notes I sent you. Send it to me tonight, and don't mention this to my dad, at least not yet. I want to figure out all the pros and cons first." Ben was about to hang up as he crossed the street, getting more amped up about possibly seeing Jenna again. "And call the realtor and have her continue showing the place. I haven't ruled out selling just yet."

Ben hung up and entered the cafe as frantic energy buzzed in his system. He scanned the entire cafe and didn't see the Jenna lookalike anywhere.

"What the hell?" he whispered as he held his hand to the back of his neck, rubbing the tension out. "This is insane," he muttered.

He pulled his phone out and dialed Dr. Archer's personal number. "This is Ben Sanderson. Please call me back. I'm hallucinating again."

Ben searched the area again. There were only four other patrons in the place, and the woman wasn't one of them. Ben placed his hand on the back of a chair, feeling lightheaded all of a sudden.

Walter came out from behind the ordering station and placed his hand on Ben's shoulder. "Everything alright? You look like you're about to drop."

"I'm not sure." Ben passed his hand through his hair, took a deep breath, and felt himself waver. Walter pulled out the chair and practically sat Ben down. He walked away and came back with a bottle of water.

"It seems to me you're looking for something? Anything I can do to help?"

"No." Ben opened the water and drained it. His lightheadedness cleared some.

"I think that I have overworked myself for so long that now that I have free time, I'm going mad." Ben laughed half-heartedly.

"Well, that is no way to be feeling, son. I heard you'll be in town for the next three months. If you get bored I could always use a hand. Melissa somehow talked me into letting her use the back portion of my building, and I got suckered into the clean-up crew."

Ben sighed, feeling exhausted all of a sudden. "I may take you up on that. Isn't there a saying that idle hands make idle minds?"

Walter got up and came back fairly quickly with another bottle of water.

"It's pretty slow in here right now, and Beth Ann has the register. I'm a good listener if you need someone to talk to."

"No, I'm good, not much you can do anyway. Unfortunately, I'm the one who has to stop chasing the ghost of the love of my life who keeps showing up around every corner."

Walter put his hand on Ben's shoulder. "Was that what you were looking for? No wonder you looked near frantic. I'm sorry, son. If you don't mind telling, how did she die?"

Ben flustered. "No, no, she isn't dead, or I hope she isn't."

Walter sat back in the chair and dropped his hand from Ben's shoulder to the table. "Well, then I'm a bit confused."

"Honestly, Walter, me too. I've been seeing my therapist for the last few years about this. For some reason, anytime I'm over-whelmed or stressed, my psyche plays tricks on me and I see the girl I loved and left all over the place. The thing is, she has never really been there. I just think I see her. My therapist thinks it's my way of coping because that time of my life was before every-thing changed, when I was carefree to dream."

"Ben, as I live and breathe, I'm getting old, nearly seventy-five, and I'm still not too old to dream. Son, you can't let your dreams die."

Ben looked up at Walter and saw something in Walter's eyes that led him to start talking.

"I met the most amazing girl my last year in college up north. She was bouncy and full of spirit, and being around her took the stress of college and life away. She breathed life I never knew I was missing into me. An unusual girl full of life, and just being near her was like I could breathe again. Something about her playfulness and sweet Southern charm reminded me of home."

Walter leaned forward and propped his chin on his hand. "Ah, young love. How did you meet her?"

"When we first met, it was by pure accident. I was rushing and not watching where I was going and completely knocked her over. All our things went flying. I hurriedly helped her up then picked up her belongings. She was gracious and blew it off, laughing at my embarrassment. When I heard her silky voice, it had that smooth Southern grace to it that I missed so much while away at school. I missed home, but there she stood with laughter practically oozing out of her even though some stranger nearly knocked her out. I wanted to talk more, but her bus arrived, and she jumped on and waved with a twinkle in her eye and a laugh. I must have looked like a complete dope standing there, open-mouthed, gaping like a fool. You would have thought I'd been the one knocked over and suffering from a concussion or something."

"Ah, the love-at-first-sight syndrome, it sure does give you a wallop."

Ben watched Walter's eyes mist up with his own memories. "You've experienced this too?"

"I sure did. My journey was a difficult one. But I knew the moment I saw him that he was for me. But back in the eighties, things were a bit more secretive, a bit more difficult. How I wish we grew up in today's world. But one thing's for certain: I never gave up hope of experiencing that feeling one more time. But enough about me. I want to hear about how this girl who got away got found again."

Ben smiled. "She left me a clue."

"Ah, intrigue." Walter rubbed his hands together. "What did she leave?"

"When she handed me the stack of large envelopes that I dropped, a pen was wedged between them. It had the name and address of a local coffee shop."

"Ah, a coffee lover, a girl after my own heart." Walter patted his chest with his hand dramatically.

"After mine as well. I lived on coffee back then and was in that shop daily. It was near campus. I made an instant decision that I would go to the coffee shop in between every class every day and stay in the evenings until I could meet up with her again."

"How long did it take for you to find her?"

Ben laughed. "Not long at all. It was like fate wanted us to meet. The next morning, I literally knocked into her again."

Walter chuckled. "More like fate was giving you a big ole shove, son."

Ben laughed too. "You are probably right. She was the first girl I met in Manhattan that even piqued my interest. I was consumed with school back then and didn't focus on anything else until her."

"So, how did the mystery girl take to getting knocked over again?" Walter asked after he took a sip of the coffee Beth Ann had brought him.

"She was cool. We had both ordered the same coffee. She left before I could think of a way to introduce myself. The following day I ran into her again as she was leaving. She laughed and shouted, 'Serendipity!' Then she grabbed my hand, tapped it to her shoulder, and said, 'You're supposed to say tag, you're it.' And turned away, laughing.

"There was something about her that made my mind muddled, and I tried to catch up to her words and actions. When I finally realized she was walking out of the cafe, I ran after her and kept pace with her as she walked without saying a darn thing. I just remember her glancing at me and smiling and drinking her coffee without saying anything."

Walter chuckled. "How long did that last?"

"I missed my class and ended up in the Garment District."

They both laughed.

"Please tell me you said something."

"I did after my eyes cleared from the daze of being in the Garment District. I looked at my watch, realizing the time. I had less than thirty minutes to get to my next class, and I was panicking thinking I would never see her again if I didn't. The first thing I thought flew out my mouth: 'Same time tomorrow?'"

Walter hooted in laughter and wiped his eyes.

Ben full-on smiled, chuckling. "She must have liked my awkwardness because she pinched my cheek like an old auntie of mine and told me I was so cute, and she'd be there. I took off running, the entire way back to class felt like a dream."

"Well, how did you do the next day? Please tell me you were more verbal."

"I was, thank goodness, at least to a certain extent. It took meeting up with her another three times before I remembered to ask her name."

"Oh, Ben, you poor besotted boy. If that girl had you all twisted up before you knew her name, no wonder she is haunting you after so many years. What I'm curious about is why you and she aren't together today?"

"That is more difficult. She had a bit of bad dating the first few months of living in Manhattan and didn't want to tell me who she was, where she worked, lived, or even her phone number. So, after meeting at the coffee shop the next few mornings, talking about our interests, it turned out we loved all the same things, hung out at all the same bookstores, movie theaters, restaurants, even the same hot dog vendor, and just never ran into one another. That's when she made up the rules to the game."

"So, what was the game?"

"She called it serendipity."

Walter nodded. "I remember that movie. John Cusack was in it. I loved it."

"Yeah, I think that's what sparked the idea. So even though we made dates to meet up, we had to randomly meet at one of our favorite places five times before we could swap phone numbers. We eventually did. It took nearly four months, but by the time the day arrived, we had a date set up, and I didn't show up. My dad had a heart attack, and I flew home. When I was finally able to go back, I couldn't find her.

"I didn't get to tell her goodbye. Honestly, I stood her up

because I was so scared my dad would die before I made it home. I didn't even wait until the next day to leave. When I did make it back, she was nowhere to be found. Our serendipity ended. I guess. But ever since then, especially this time of year when I screwed up and left without a goodbye, I really miss her. Since being here, I swear I see her all over the place, but she isn't there when I follow and go where I thought she went. I guess because I don't have work to focus on, I'm hallucinating. I should probably call my therapist."

"I don't think you need to go that far, son. Sometimes when you love someone, they never leave your heart, whether the love was a few months or a few years. I remember when I was in my thirties, the love of my life left me. He couldn't handle the stress of our relationship in the small Southern town, and he was tired of not living up to his dreams and potential. I understood but didn't want to follow. I love my town and felt that the people here wouldn't judge. They never have. But there are days when I'm home alone, and I can still see Max walking around the corner. It's been thirty years and—"

Walter had looked up when the door jingled. As he stopped talking, he placed his hand over his heart and started breathing heavily, and swayed in his seat.

Ben held Walter by the elbow to prevent him from falling out of his chair. Breathing heavily, Walter gripped Ben's hand with a death grip. "Son, please tell me you see a man in a green suit walking this way." Ben turned, and walking toward them was one of the world's leading men's fashion designers. Ben actually owned one of his suits. He'd saved a year to buy it. Ben's parents always told him presentation was everything, and his mom taught him to dress well and his dad taught him to dress with pomp and circumstance in the business world. For high school graduation, his parents bought him a pair of Maximillian Thorne golden cufflinks that he wore practically every day. What could someone like him be doing in Cypressville?

"Uh, yeah, I do."

The tall man with an immaculate silver beard wore the most expensive-looking emerald green suit Ben had ever seen, and it fit to perfection. He walked to their table and sat down across from Walter. He watched Walter with the utmost concern etched across his face.

"Max, you're back."

"I am," the elegant man said, his eyes downcast. Strange how the man looked so confident in the magazines but sitting here, he seemed nearly as frail as Walter.

"For how long?"

"As long as it takes for you to forgive me."

Walter jumped up fast and nearly fell back. Ben and Max both got up quickly. Ben helped steady Walter and had his back to the door when the bell of the cafe jingled and he heard her voice. It still carried the hint of smiles and joy with each word. "Walter," she said, "I got locked out the back—"

Her tone changed, and she squealed out in glee. "Max!" She drew out the model's name. She wrapped her arms around his waist. "I can't believe it. You really came!" Jenna, the girl he'd been fantasizing over since college, was standing before him for real. Without a thought, he walked up behind her and pinched the back of her upper arm.

"Ouch." She rubbed the back of her arm as she turned toward Walter. "What the heck, Wa—" The words died on her lips. Instead of seeing Walter behind her, she saw him.

Ben's mouth was dry, and his stomach fluttered with both nerves and excitement at finally seeing Jenna again. And by the time his mind caught up with his mouth to say something, she slapped him across the face and ran out of the cafe.

CHAPTER EIGHT

*M*ax gently shook Ben's shoulder. "Boy, if you are who I think you might be, I think you best clear away those cobwebs in your brain and go after my niece."

Ben didn't hesitate and flew out the door searching for Jenna. He saw her dark ponytail swinging as she ran. He ran after her, every now and then swerving and nearly knocking people over in his haste. Why did they have to have so many people lollygagging on the sidewalk today? She ran into the monogram shop that he thought he saw her in the other day, and within seconds after her, he swung the door open, the little bell chiming in his wake.

"Jenna, please let me explain," Ben shouted in the store when he didn't see her anywhere.

"I don't want to hear what you have to say."

He followed her voice to the back of the store. He walked into the back room that looked like a breakroom.

Ben didn't know what to say other than spit out the hard facts fast. Then, the words he longed to tell her for years started coming. "Jenna, please. That night, I didn't skip out on you on purpose." He wanted to tell her that he was in love with her but figured it might all be an illusion after all these years, and he stopped himself.

"Right!" she hollered from a closed door at the back of the breakroom.

He walked to the door and leaned his forehead against it. He breathed out heavily. "My dad had a heart attack. Umma didn't know if he would make it. So, I rushed to the airport. By the time I got home from the hospital, I realized that I should have called the restaurant and had them page you or leave a message, but I didn't think. I've regretted that moment since."

Ben didn't know what else to say. He slid to the floor, sitting with his back against the door. After a few moments, Jenna spoke. "You must have been so scared. Is your dad...?" She let her word trail off in question.

"He survived. It took a while for him to recover, and by the time I went back to New York, you had moved on. The old barista we used to go to, Joe, said he hadn't seen you in months. I guess our serendipity wore out."

"I guess so."

He heard the door crack, and he slid back, opening it further as he fell backward. He caught himself on his elbows but was now mostly sprawled on the floor. Jenna stood looking down on him. His smile wavered. "Hey, long time no see."

She wiped her eyes and choked out a laugh. "I see your humor hasn't changed much."

He held his forefinger and thumb to where only a half an inch separated them. "Maybe it improved this much."

She gave a full laugh and nudged his hip with the toe of her shoe. "Want to come in?"

Ben sat up and jumped up quickly, walking into what seemed like a walk-in closet turned into a sewing room. In the far left corner was a mannequin-like thing with a dress pinned to it. On a hot pink small settee were stacks of what he figured were rolls of silks in a couple of different shades of white, and in front of a small window facing the back alleyway behind her building was a sewing machine.

Jenna walked to the settee, picked up the stack of fabric, and leaned them on the wall opposite. She sat down, patting the seat next to her with her hand. It had been so long since Ben was near her that the thought of being on the same sofa made his heart pound in his chest. It beat so forcefully that he glanced down to see if his shirt was moving in rhythm to it after he sat down.

It wasn't.

When he placed his hand over his chest and took a deep breath, Jenna's hand touched his shoulder. "You okay?"

He lifted his head. "I've dreamed of this moment since the day I left you. I can't stop my heart from pounding, and now that you aren't kicking me out, I don't know what to say."

Jenna moved her hand and placed both between her knees. "It's strange. For a second, it felt like old times, but now I feel awkward."

"Same."

"For the record, I've thought about you too."

They both sat in silence for what felt like an eternity before Jenna finally spoke. "I was an idiot for playing that game. I wish I had given you my number. Actually, I was planning on giving it that night, but…"

"Yeah, I screwed that night up. I wish I had thought to call the restaurant. So many wasted years."

Jenna rocked back and forth for a minute, then leaned back on the sofa, resting the back of her head on the headrest. "Ben, can I ask you something?"

"Sure."

"Want to go get some ice cream? All this is stressing me out."

Ben laughed as relief swept through him. He turned serious again and lifted some of the long dark hair from her shoulder, rubbing the silky texture between his fingers. "You haven't changed a bit, just as beautiful, and honestly, I'd love some ice cream. It'll be my treat."

J enna bounced up with nervous energy. Horses galloped in circles inside her stomach at being so near Ben again. Millions of questions swirled in her head. Why was he in Cypressville? What had he been doing the last eight years? Did he live nearby? Could it be possible that he and Melissa both lived in New Orleans for a while? There were many times when Jenna would make a weekend trip to visit Melissa and could have sworn, she'd seen Ben. But, all these years, she just thought it was her mind playing tricks or a Ben lookalike. She wanted to ask, but she felt shy rather than outgoing for the first time in ages.

Her heart had broken so badly after he no-showed for the date that when she came home, it took nearly a year to start healing. She had loved him and was so angry at her childish behavior, making him play stupid games. She had wished over and over that she would have trusted him sooner and given him her number. When she thought about it over the years, she realized that she knew she could trust him after two weeks, but she was having fun with the anonymity and playing the game so she let it go on for nearly four months.

"I haven't had ice cream in town yet. Which way is it?" Ben interrupted her thoughts as he held the door open for her.

Jenna stepped out, walking left out of her shop. He followed close behind her. "We'll have to take my car. The best place is out of town. One of the local farmers' wives got bored when all her kids left for college, and she made some of the most amazing ice creams. She set up a small old-time ice cream parlor on the property.

"That sounds cool."

"It is."

They walked only a few paces before she stopped at a silver Honda. "This is me, the door's unlocked." She pointed to the car as she walked over to the driver's side.

As Ben climbed in, he seemed so large and scrunched in her car compared to her.

"The lever under the seat will give you more legroom."

He stretched out his legs a bit more, and she watched him feel for the sidebar to lower the seat back. He turned to her and smiled as he buckled his seatbelt. "I'm ready."

She felt like a deer in headlights looking at his smile. She'd forgotten how it used to make her heart sputter when she could get him to grace her with it. When they first met, he had been so serious all the time. Once she saw his smile the first time, she worked double-time to make him continually repeat it. Her memories weren't as great as reality. Sitting in his presence once again turned her into a mushy pile of goo. Ben was beyond beautiful. At thirty-one, he had lost youth of the young college boy she dated. His body filled out his clothes in just the right way, his jaw was well defined, and he had little crow's feet just beginning to develop, even a few silver strands of hair speckled through his dark black hair. Her mouth practically filled with drool staring at him.

Uncle Max would probably want to steal him away to model his suits with his muscled, broad shoulders and narrow waist, and she'd forgotten how tall he was, or had he grown more? A vision of her jumping on his back and spinning around in circles infiltrated her thoughts.

A smile flew to her lips at the vision. Jenna loved not only that he was tall, but that he was sturdy. She felt safe having fun and being playful, especially with her being a little heavier than the average, knowing that when she jumped on his back, it wouldn't break. He would just heft her up and carry her around the park as if she were light as a feather. It always gave her a strange sense of power and security, which never made sense to her, but when she would rest her cheek on his back, she felt like there was nothing in the world she couldn't achieve.

How many times had she nearly broken her promise to herself that she wouldn't get carried away only to get burned, by telling him who she was in those moments?

His fingers snapped before her eyes. "Earth to Jenna." She shook her head to try and focus but was about to get lost in her ogling again when he said, "Do you need me to drive?"

She forced herself to stop looking at him and turned the key in the ignition. "I'm good. It's just been a bit of a shocking day, to say the least."

"I can't argue with that. Do you want to know a secret?"

After she pulled out of the parking spot, she glanced at him out of the corner of her eye. "Heck, yeah," she said in the fakest happy voice she could muster. Then turned a bit more serious. "But I better forewarn you, these days I can't keep a secret to save my soul. So, you'll have to make sure it's something you don't mind everyone knowing."

He made a smothered laughing sound.

"I'm being serious. Since I came home, somehow, I became the town gossip, sticking my nose in everyone's business so that I didn't have to remember mine."

Jenna threw her hand over her mouth immediately and dropped it just as quickly. Why did she confess that? The energy in the car became stifling, and she chanced another side look at Ben. His eyes were downcast, he couldn't seem to look at her, and all expression seemed to have disappeared from his face. She knew that expression all too well. She saw it in the mirror most mornings before she did her mantras to put what she called 'her happy' on.

Depression and guilt were written all over it, and she hated that he seemed to carry some of the same burdens she did.

"See, I can't even keep my own secrets," she chirped in her most bubbly voice, hoping he'd buy her fake cheeriness like everyone else did.

"Jenna, you don't have to fake it for me. I get it. I screwed up. I've regretted it every moment since I got on the plane to come home."

"Ben." Jenna's voice broke on his name. Tears started to leak out of her eyes without warning, and then even worse, she felt a colossal sob break through. Jenna knew she couldn't keep driving and immediately pulled over in the next parking lot and parked. The second she stopped, the waterworks started to overflow, and she covered her face with her hands as she broke out into the most gut-wrenching sobs she had since he abandoned her all those years ago.

Before long, she felt Ben shift in the car, unfasten his seat belt and hers, and somehow got her in his arms, hugging her while she cried on his shoulder. "I'm so sorry," he kept whispering over and over and over until she finally stopped crying.

"No, Ben, it's not your fault. It's mine. It was all my idea, my plan to play the dumb game, and I carried it on too long. By week two, I was ready to give you my number, but I didn't. I was too slow, too childish, and kept it going. Finally, that night I was done with my games and had the stupid coffee shop pen with my number written on it." She started crying again.

He hugged her tighter, and his voice broke. "I was going to tell you I loved you." That was when he broke down, making her cry even harder.

He had loved her.

CHAPTER NINE

*T*wo days passed, and Jenna hadn't seen Ben. After their breakdown in the car, she had bailed on the ice cream, embarrassed, and told him she was ready just to go home. She knew he needed the release from so many unanswered questions when he wiped his eyes just like she did. It sort of caught her off guard. She never saw a man cry and felt awkward as he wiped his eyes. She politely asked him to leave so she could go home and figure out her feelings. She was so out of her element, and she knew Max would bombard her with questions the second he caught up with her.

Ben seemed understanding as he got out of her car and thanked her for listening.

She nodded, focusing on the car in front of her, suddenly overwhelmed and trying to harden her heart so as not to seem so vulnerable and ready to jump into his arms as if no time had passed. And like a fool, she started her car and took off, even though half of her wanted to ask him to stay and never leave again.

Once she got home, the only thing Max said to her before

helping her cut the pattern for Melissa's gown was, "Was his explanation valid?"

Jenna nodded, and that was it.

It wasn't until she was in bed that night that she realized they didn't exchange numbers again. After staying up half the night berating herself, she figured, why would they? It wasn't like he was asking her to start over. He just wanted to clear his name. Then she got angry at him for not calling the restaurant. It would have solved so much heartache.

This morning she woke up feeling better than she had in ages. Knowing Ben's reasons and forgiving him brought a sense of relief at first. Then the anxiety returned. She once again regretted not getting his number and feared she'd never see him again. The only thing she could think of was finding him. She had to get his last name, at least, if he didn't want to share his number.

Jenna closed her shop for the day and roamed the entire town searching for him. Six hours passed with no luck. She couldn't understand how she, the town gossip, the girl who could get any information out of anyone in town, failed to find anyone who had seen him.

Walter had been sick the last two days, and when she tried to bring him soup to possibly get info out of him, he told her to leave it at the door and wouldn't see her. Disheartened, she left it and went to the B and B and got stuck sitting with the owner, Jane, for two hours having the most boring tea of her life, only to be told Ben checked out the day before.

Jenna got back into her car and noticed that her phone had forty-seven messages and six missed calls from Melissa. Her stomach flipped over in fear that something horrible had happened. Then, as she was about to press Melissa's number, her name flashed on the screen, ringing again.

"Mel, everything okay?"

Melissa was frantic, and her words were flying out of her mouth at lightning speed, not in fear but anger and frustration.

Two words stood out loud and clear: dinner and best man. She looked at the clock on the dashboard. It was six thirty-eight. She was over a half-hour late.

"Shoot, I'm sorry. I was distracted and—"

Melissa interrupted Jenna's excuses. Even with all the background noise, Jenna could hear the warble of relief in Melissa's voice. Jenna felt like the worst friend of the century. She knew Melissa didn't do well when the people she loved didn't respond to calls or texts right away. Melissa was still trying to heal over the loss of her mom, and after Jake got sick with pneumonia and was in the hospital in January, her anxieties ran high. Thank goodness he was an overall strong and healthy man who recovered in a little over a week.

"I'm so sorry I worried you. I promise it wasn't on purpose. I left my phone in the car, and Jane kept me longer than I expected."

Melissa started on with a rant about being stuck at Jane's yesterday. Jenna listened for a few seconds as disappointment in herself began to crop up about how she had forgotten her best friend in a few hours. This incident proved she should stop looking for Ben. It wasn't meant to be. If it were, he would have never left her.

His return wasn't healthy for her. He was too all-consuming. He was like that back then too. That's why when he stood her up, she fell into such a deep depression, a depression that came back every year at the same time he left her, the same time she finally moved home, and any time she saw someone who looked like him. She struggled to live life without him. She struggled with this aspect of her personality. You shouldn't need someone so badly. She worked so hard to learn to be happy without him in her life, and now he was back.

Jenna took a deep breath deciding that she'd forgive Ben and let him go this time. Now that she knew his reasons, she had closure. She whispered, "That's all I need."

Melissa heard her. Instead of explaining what she had said, she brought the topic back to why Melissa called. "Do you still want me to meet y'all at the restaurant? It will probably take me at least twenty to get there."

Jenna probably also pushed the dinner out of her head because she didn't want to meet the best man this early on in the wedding prep, knowing good and well it was on purpose to try and get her to fall for him. She had no desire for the matchmaking session Melissa and Jake were both clearly trying to arrange with her and Jake's best friend. Both of them had been talking him up over the last few weeks.

"I have to run home to throw on my dress, and then I'll be there." She counted the time to her house, to change, and the drive to the restaurant. "Give me twenty minutes."

As Melissa was about to hang up, Jenna stopped her. "Mel, I'm sorry. I'll make it up to you, I promise."

Melissa ended the call with, "You better."

Jenna should have put alerts on her phone to remind her, mainly because of Mel's anxiety, but the other reason was that she tended to be a control freak with planning. Everything always had to run smoothly. Even though she had made the Christmas festival and her dad's wedding so unique that the influencers were still posting about it and she kept getting tons of requests to plan events all over the country, she'd been a bit obsessive over anything and everything she plans.

It usually did run smoothly, but Melissa always second-guessed herself now since she screwed up two Christmases ago on the Governor's Ball and didn't thoroughly check everything over. Now because of it, she was a stickler for triple-checking her list.

"Crud," Jenna groaned as she started the car and sped home. She didn't feel like meeting Jake's friend, but then she laughed. She would make herself entirely undesirable for this guy. Instead of going home, she pulled up in front of her shop. She ran to the back room, grabbed one of the designs she created a few months ago, and slipped the deep red dress on. She made it for Melissa but put it on anyway. It was the wrong fit for her, a little too snug in the waist and hips. The chest area was too loose around her bust, and the bottom was too tight over her hips and lower stomach. She rubbed her hands over the pudge, making a wrinkle line across her lower abdomen. She smiled at her reflection, at how perfectly unflattering the dress was, and prayed it worked to keep her from looking appealing to this guy. She kept her flip-flops on, showing off her chipped toenail polish, to complete the ensemble. She pulled her hair out of the ponytail, fluffed it in the mirror without brushing it, and then applied a deep red lipstick that made her look ghostly pale. Some found it attractive because of the stark differences, but she thought it made her look sick. For the final pièce de résistance, she put on patchouli, knowing that it was a hit or miss scent with some people. Hoping the best man was one of the misses, she doused herself in the potent oil.

Jenna arrived at the restaurant in record time, practically throwing her keys to the valet as she rushed in.

Flushed and panting, she gulped deep breaths of air, waving to Melissa as she spotted her across the room at the bar. They had waited for her to arrive to be seated. The tension showed in Melissa's brows. She was worried, and Jake rubbed her shoulders, not even looking at her as he spoke to his best man who was obscured from her vision.

Melissa met her halfway and grabbed her elbow, pulling her toward Jake and the best man. "What in the world is going on with you? You have been out of it the last two days! Now, ignoring my calls and now an hour late. I mean, seriously, are you upset with me or something?"

Jenna was surprised, "Goodness no! Don't even think that. It's just I've been struggling again the last couple of days like I did when I came home from New York."

Melissa's eyes immediately tilted down, and her hand clasped her wrist gently. "Oh Jenna, I'm so sorry. If this is too much for you, we could postpone it."

"Don't you dare feel sorry for me, Mel. I'll get over it." Jenna placed a huge fake smile on her lips. "See? I'm good."

"Liar, but thanks. We can make it quick and just get appetizers if you'd like. I doubt the boys would mind. I think they would have both preferred a hamburger compared to coming here, but I wanted to try it out. This new little restaurant is a big contender for my reception."

"Really? I thought you were going with Chez François?"

"I was until François called telling me he had to head back to France. His brother decided to get married and picked the same day."

"Dang, bad timing."

"Exactly, and this is one of the only places that can take on a last-minute wedding. I have two other places to check out over the next few days."

"Which places?"

"Antoine's and Jack's Bar-B-Q."

Jenna laughed. "Barbeque?"

Melissa looked like she'd sucked a lemon at the thought of having a barbeque at her wedding.

"Jake and Megan picked it, and when I told Jake no, instantly Megan's face dropped as if I shot down all her dreams in one shot."

Jenna laughed, thinking of how bossy Jake's little niece could be, "You folded to a five-year-old. Why search any further? We all know what's going to happen."

"No! It will not, but I will let them believe I am considering it by going for a taste test."

Jenna stopped walking the moment she saw Jake talking to his best man. She couldn't believe it. All her searching, anxiety over if she would see him again, and all along, Ben was standing there beside Jake laughing at something he said. His almond-shaped eyes still crinkled, practically disappearing when he laughed heartily. She hadn't noticed that his dark hair was longer than it had been back in college. How had she not noticed the other day? She clearly remembered him tucking it behind his ear, but it didn't even click? Even though she had dark brown hair, she always envied his thick black strands that always shimmered blue in specific lighting.

Melissa curled back under the weight of Jake's arm. "Ben, I'd like for you to meet my best friend and bridesmaid, Jenna."

CHAPTER TEN

*B*en couldn't believe the maid of honor was Jenna. In his head, he had created the worst sort of woman. He had watched Jake over the past thirty minutes rub circles on Melissa's back each time she texted and got no response. Melissa kept giving Ben some sort of pleading look as she stared at her phone for the umpteenth time. "She normally isn't like this," she had said in the process of calling her bridesmaid once more and finally reaching her. She had stepped away from the table, but Ben noticed the tension leave Melissa's shoulders the second her friend answered.

Jake had confided in Ben that Melissa tended to get anxious about the people she loved if they didn't answer right away since her mom passed away. Her dog, Snickerdoodle, who was usually with her, kept her calm, but she left the dog with her dad and his new wife to pet-sit this evening.

He was expecting a snotty woman who thought more of herself than her best friend. Never in a million years would he have imagined Jenna to turn into someone who didn't care enough about her best friend to at least call or text to say she'd be late.

He had very little patience for people being late and even less for those without consideration. On top of all of that, he was starting to feel embarrassed because of crying yesterday with her.

Jake interrupted his thoughts by clearing his throat, and without thinking, Ben spat out, "Nice to meet you."

Jenna's eyes squinted, and she took a shaky breath that nearly sunk her chest inward as if she were physically punched. Before he could rectify it, she turned to Jake. "I'm so sorry I'm late. Not only is Max in town helping me with Mel's gown, but I also had a rough couple of days. I had my phone on silent earlier and forgot to turn it back on, and I completely lost track of time. I know it doesn't mean much, but I am sorry."

"No worries."

Jake gave her a side hug as the waiter arrived.

The dinner was awkward. Jake and Melissa kept trying to get Ben and Jenna to talk, but it was futile. He'd screwed up when he greeted her as if she were a stranger and she was now giving him the cold shoulder. Obviously, he hurt her feelings. She wouldn't look at him all night. He kept internally fighting with himself. Just because Jenna looked the same didn't mean she was the same person he fell in love with back in college.

She was a different woman and made excuses for being an hour late to her best friend's event. When she wasn't looking, he kept glancing at her, watching her interactions with Melissa and Jake. Jenna seemed way more reserved than he remembered. Even though initially he thought she looked the same, she had grown more beautiful. Her cheekbones seemed a little more prominent and her body a little fuller, softer. Her skin glowed in the candlelight at the table, and he couldn't seem to take his eyes off those full red lips, remembering what they felt like on his.

Each time a thought like that popped up into his mind, he had to remind himself that both of them had probably changed so much and that she wasn't the same girl as back then. Then she pulled the cherry out of her coke, put it in her mouth, and twirled the stem. He nearly jumped out of his seat when she glanced at him and winked just like she used to when they would meet up back in college. He had no idea why she did it now; it's not like they were kids again. What was she thinking?

"Jenna!" his mind had been so consumed by her that he didn't realize he shouted her name, interrupting the conversation at the table. Everyone looked at him as if he were some kind of pariah.

When he didn't say anything, Jenna removed the stem. "Yeah?" she asked all innocently. Was she paying him back, trying to get a rise out of him? Make him remember who she was to him and mock him with it? Was she that cold now? Ben had always been the quieter and more conservative type, whereas Jenna was always humming, moving, playing, smiling, laughing, teasing him, and constantly lifting his spirits when he became too serious.

Jake's hand squeezed his shoulder. "Ben, you look a little flushed. Are you alright?"

"I uh, I need to step outside for a minute. I was going to ask Jenna if she would like to join me for a walk on the back patio so we can get to know one another a bit." He stood up, placed his cloth napkin on the table, stepped over to Jenna's seat, and held his hand out.

Glancing at Melissa, she practically was bouncing in her seat with a smile so wide he had a feeling that she was hoping that he would like her friend. Jake had a knowing look as well. Jenna, on the other hand, started to fidget with her fork next to her half-eaten steak. He could see Melissa's hand shove Jenna's under the table. Jenna put her lips to her glass of wine and before she realized it, it was empty. Nothing was standing in her way of accepting his hand.

When her soft hand clasped his, his mind raced with the thought of never letting her go. He shifted her hand to the crook of his elbow, guiding her out of the restaurant.

"You look beautiful tonight."

Before she could say anything, she hiccupped. Ben gave her a side glance. When she opened her mouth to try and talk again, she hiccupped again. When they reached the small boardwalk near the pond behind the restaurant, they sat on a bench facing the water. When Jenna tried to talk again, the hiccup made a burp sound. Her face flushed, and she buried her face in her hands and started shaking.

Was she crying?

Then she moved her hands and tilted her head back, laughing and hiccupping at the same time. He couldn't help but join in as the tension once more broke between them.

"I'm sorry for treating you like a stranger when you arrived. I had just played up her maid of honor to be some horrible human being and was pretty shocked to see you standing there."

Jenna took a few deep breaths, trying to stop her hiccups. "Remind me never to drink coke that fast again."

"Does that mean I'm forgiven?"

"Who says you were forgiven the first time?"

Ben froze. He purposely hadn't gone searching for her for the last two days because he wanted her to have some time to adjust to seeing him after all these years. He figured that after their crying session, she might need some time to take it all in. He had hoped that she accepted his apology and understood all the reasons why he didn't show up to dinner all those years ago.

"Don't look so shocked. I'm just joking. I'm not an ogre or anything. I understand now why you didn't meet me. It was all horrible timing. Who knows, Ben? If we had gotten even more serious back then, maybe we would have had some issues or something. I know I needed to grow up some. That experience made me realize how childish I was. If it didn't happen, who knows how utterly ridiculous I would be today."

"Jenna, you were not childish back then. You may have had a youthful spirit, but that part of you was like sunshine to my soul.

I'm too serious, and meeting you has helped me shine in ways I never knew possible. I certainly hope you didn't bury that too deeply."

Jenna leaned back on the bench and tilted her face to the stars. She sniffed. Ben saw a lone tear slide out the corner of her eye.

"Ben," Jenna whispered his name as she reached for his hand and squeezed it in her own. "How is it that when we are alone like this, it feels as if no time has passed. Your presence makes me feel like this is where I'm supposed to be, but I keep telling myself that really, I don't know you anymore."

Ben leaned into her. "I've been thinking the same exact thing."

Jenna lifted her head and turned toward him. "Can I tell you something without you getting upset with me?"

"Of course." Ben's curiosity spiked. What in the world could Jenna tell him that would make him upset with her?

"I never told anyone we ever dated. I'm glad you reacted the way you did when we met. I don't want anyone to know that we ever dated."

Ben sat up straighter. How had she never talked about him? He has told literally everyone, even Walter, a man he practically just met, about the girl he left behind.

"What? Why?" was all he could spit out.

"Well, like the game, back then, I didn't want to tell anyone about you because I wanted to make sure it would last. Before you, I dated many guys who only liked me for an in with my uncle. He picked on me all the time that I was too easy. So, when I met you, although certain how adorable you were the first time we met, I didn't want to deal with the teasing, so the purpose of the game was to develop a real bond, hopefully."

Ben muttered under his breath, "Well, that happened for me."

Jenna ignored him and continued with her explanation. She could tell Ben was upset over her not talking about him. "Once I was certain, or fate took control, we'd share everything. I mean, I told you some of that but not my real reasons, I guess. But when you left, I was glad I never told anyone I was seeing you. It was easier never to have to talk about it to anyone and be reminded of the man who dumped me."

"I didn't dump you," Ben said through gritted teeth, aggravated that she could just pretend he didn't exist when all he had thought about, dreamed about, and had hours of therapy about, was his grief over never seeing her again. Yet, she could just think of him as a passing memory. He stood up and started to walk away.

"You said you wouldn't get upset," Jenna shouted, making him stop in his tracks.

He turned around. "How can I not be upset, Jenna, when the woman I loved...used to love, and have compared every woman to, has basically told me to my face I don't exist?"

He turned around and started to stalk off when she grabbed his arm. She was stronger than he gave her credit when his arm twisted back in her grip.

"What?" he snapped.

"I never said you didn't exist. If it makes you feel any better, you're the man I compare every single other man to. I loved you too. I was going to tell you that night at the restaurant. And no one, and I mean no one has ever come close to making my heart sing like it did when I was with you."

Ben gave her a questioning stare, doubting her words for only a moment. Her heart shined in her eyes. He knew she was telling the truth, but it must have taken his features a while to show it because she started trying to persuade him more.

"I'm serious. You can ask Melissa how many men I've dated since I came home if you don't believe me."

His curiosity piqued, his mouth asked the question before his brains could stop him. "How many men have you dated?"

"I went to dinner with three men. Dinner, Ben, nothing ever went beyond one flipping date. I couldn't handle being with any of them. What about you?" All the fire went out of her. Jenna looked exhausted, and even so, her words lifted his heart.

Ben couldn't hold in his smile. "Same."

The moments of talking about the past were so much easier than contemplating what their future could be. Would he even like this new Jenna? Both of them had probably changed so much it wasn't fair of him to try and pick up where things left off. Plus, it seems like even if he wanted to, he couldn't. No one here even knew they existed as a couple except for maybe her uncle, who seemed to know a little something when he sent Ben after her the other day. "So, another game, huh? You want me to pretend we never met."

"Yep."

Ben chuckled to cover up the hurt he felt from her still wanting to hide knowing him. He hoped she would have been past playing games, seeing how bad the first time went. But maybe this was her way of not wanting to move forward in getting to know one another. Seriously, if she wanted to, she'd surely ask for his number. Well, he wouldn't volunteer it. If she wanted to play strangers, he'd play strangers, then when the wedding was over, he'd go home to bury himself in trying to save the family business.

He was too old for this. He only had to play along for another month before he could go home and back to normal. At least he got to apologize. Dr. Archer told him that it was good he found her. It would give him closure, help him move forward, and not look back anymore. He hoped she was right.

He took a deep breath and tried to make his voice and facial expressions seem indifferent and unaffected by how hurt he felt inside. "Well, in a way, this is probably good. It's been nearly eight years since we've seen each other. In fact, to me, that does make us strangers. I know I have changed." He looked her up and down. Even in the ill-fitting dress and messy hair, he still thought she was beautiful. She had filled out, and he loved that Jenna was still just as confident in herself as she had been back then. "And you have too."

Her eyes widened, and her cheeks flared to life with color. Did he embarrass her? He could hear her teeth grind. Did he offend her? How? It's not like what he said wasn't the truth. They both had changed in the last eight years. No one stays the same.

Jenna stood up straighter, and her chin jutted out. "Yeah, I have changed."

Ben couldn't figure out what made her all bristly all of a sudden. "We'll, most likely run into each other now that I'm in town, it's as good an excuse as any to help us get reacquainted. That is, if you want to, or would you rather me keep my distance until this is all over?"

Jenna put her finger to her lips. Her eyes seemed to be contemplating the idea. "Hmm, I don't know."

Ben gulped, and his mouth became parched. Had she turned into a tease? First, she looked mad, now seductive. How could he be such a fool to still be in love with her? He felt stupid, just moments ago hoping he could move forward, and within seconds he was dreaming again that they could pick up where they left off. His therapist warned him that he needed to stop that fantasy and be more realistic, but he still hoped that she would love him if he did.

His dad always called him a dreamer. Maybe that's why his dad struggled to let him run the company. Perhaps he thought that Ben didn't have the know-how to live beyond the dream.

Jenna put her finger on the center of his brows, interrupting his deep thoughts. "What are you thinking?"

He felt his head unconsciously move back and knock her finger away.

"Still so serious." She placed her hands on his upper arms and shook him a bit. "I was only joking. There is no backing out now. We have to at least try to get to know one another again. Those two went out of their way to introduce us." She pointed to the restaurant where Jake and Melissa were probably wondering what was taking them so long.

"Anyway, it would be weird if we ignored each other. I don't want to make any part of Melissa's wedding a drama. She deserves her day to be as special as she tries to make everyone else's."

At first, Ben couldn't figure out what she was going on about because he was lost in his thoughts about work and his dad, then it all came rushing back. Her new game. At least he didn't have to ignore her.

"Come on." She linked her arm with his. "Don't want the two lovebirds to think we fell into the lake."

After a few steps, Jenna stopped and groaned.

"What?"

Jenna started laughing.

"What's so funny?"

Ben started to think Jenna might have had a little too much wine, then realized she only drank a coke through dinner. She didn't stop laughing. If anything, she started to laugh harder when he looked at her like she was bonkers. When she snorted, Ben's mood lightened. He couldn't help but join in her laughter at who knows what.

He then remembered, she used to do this out of the blue all the time, laugh at something only she knew, and bring him along for the ride. It always eased his stress like a balm to sore muscles. She could find humor in the oddest things and always pull him in when he became too serious. It was one of the things he fell in love with back then, and he could feel himself wanting to fall in love with her again even though he knew he shouldn't.

She was bent over with her hands on her knees, the laughter slowly dying away and getting more and more in control. Finally, she took a deep breath and stood up straight again, wiping her eyes.

"Melissa has been trying to set me up on blind dates with you forever. Do you know, not once has she ever called you by name?"

"What did she call me?"

"Jake's friend, Jake's boss, the best man. She told me the minute she met you. She knew we would hit it off. There was something about you that had Jenna written all over it."

Ben chuckled in disbelief.

"Dear lord, she knows me so well. If only she knew how well and right she was about you."

"You could tell her the truth, you know. We don't have to pretend." For a brief second, his hopes lifted then dropped just as quickly when Jenna sobered up and her expression changed. She looked practically horrified at that thought.

"I can't. It would hurt her feelings to know that I kept you a secret all these years."

"I can't say that I understand your logic, but I will respect your wishes. We will pretend to be perfect strangers getting to know one another like any respective friends of the bride and groom would."

Jenna's face went white, making the deep red lipstick look nearly black in contrast. "Does Jake know? Oh my gosh, if he knows, then he will tell Melissa, and she will never forgive me. Ben, what did you tell Jake about me?"

Jenna looked like she was about to be sick. Ben had to think fast, trying to remember what he told Jake.

"I think you're safe. If I recall, I stopped using your name years ago because it hurt too much to say it, so when talking about you, I always called you my lost love."

Jenna blew out a breath she was holding in relief. "Let's go in, we've been out here long enough, and I'm tired. It's been a long day."

CHAPTER ELEVEN

*J*enna walked into her shop toting two cups of espresso. She walked up to Max and handed him one as he sat behind the counter next to one of her monogram machines. "Thanks for watching the shop for me. I'm starting to worry about Walter. He's never sick, and he won't come to the door when I bring him soup or try to check in on him."

Max's head popped up fast, and concern laced his voice. "Walt is sick? When did this happen?"

Confused at Max's reaction, Jenna said, "About a week and a half ago now." Max's brows lifted, and he stood up and started pacing behind the counter like he did when he had a project that was giving him grief.

Then it dawned on her. It didn't register right away because she was so happy to see Max, but now she remembered it was the next day after his appearance in the cafe that Walter was out sick and hadn't been back since. Did that have to do with Max's return?

"Max, by any chance, would Walter be the man you left when you moved to Manhattan?"

He turned sharply to her and breathed out. "Yes, I decided to be brave and get the first meeting over with. I thought doing it in public would be easier. I swear I was fearful I gave the old fool a heart attack. So, after I told the young man, who I assumed was the one that made you decide to move back home based on your reaction, I sent him after you and tried to talk to Walter, but he just got up, took off his apron, and walked out of the cafe."

Jenna placed her hand over Max's forearm. "Oh Max, I'm so sorry. It seems we all abandoned you on your first day into town. What a horrible welcome reception you got."

He patted her hand with his. "It will be alright. Walter deserves his anger and distance. I don't think he's sick like you think. I believe he is processing me being back in town, and you, my darling, are too close to me. I did wrong by him, and honestly, I still don't forgive myself for the way I ended things. I, like your young man, took off without a goodbye, and back then before cell phones, our numbers changed when we moved, so Walter had no way of getting in touch with me. It was all up to me to contact him, and I didn't. He knew we were over. Eventually, I became famous, and he knew where to find me just as I knew where to find him. Neither of us took the initiative to call the other. I didn't blame him, of course. Why would he look for me when I took off in the middle of the night without a trace, with no warning?"

Jenna's heart sank. Max's story sounded eerily similar to hers. Poor Walter must have felt very similar to how she did, but she knew Max was a good man. He never had a relationship with anyone her entire life, so she believed he preferred to be alone. Never did she imagine he would still be in love with someone after so long not seeing them. It had to be, what, going on thirty years?

"Regardless, Max. I can see with my own two eyes that you care for him after all these years. Walter has been the same man my entire life. He can't be very different than when you knew him. I'm sure you can make amends."

"Jenna, darling, it's been too long. We are both completely different men today. It would be an unbelievable dream for me even to conceive the notion that he and I were still compatible."

Jenna's stomach churned as her chest tightened. Max was right. For her and Ben, eight years was a long time. Even Ben had said they were both very different people. She berated herself mentally for once again being such a kid to believe that they could fall in love again. She hugged her uncle and said into his shoulder, "But is it wrong to still dream?"

Max squeezed her. "No, darling, we wouldn't be human if we didn't."

He pulled away, picked his espresso back up off the counter where he placed it earlier, and headed to the back. "Let's get to work on this dress. We have over five thousand tiny pearls to hand stitch on today."

Jenna stretched out her arms over her head, wiggling her fingers, then did a few body stretches as if training for the Olympics. Max chuckled at her over-exaggeration of prepping to sew. Jenna plopped down in her chair, picked up the needle and thread, and groaned as she dug out the first tiny pearl. "Ugh, why did I have to talk Melissa into adding her mom's pearls into the design?"

"Because you are an amazing friend, and this dress will be stunning on Melissa. When she came for her fitting yesterday, she would have cried if you wouldn't have fussed at her."

Jenna laughed. "That's because if she cried, she would have swooned onto the settee and undone all the pins I placed on the dress to create that perfect look you keep going on about."

The bell to the shop chimed, and Jenna stepped into the front, shouting, "Welcome!"

"Jenna, how lovely to see you again." Blair, the YouTube and TikTok influencer, came striding forward with Melissa and

Snickerdoodle in tow. Jenna gave Melissa a sharp stare that said, *What the heck?*

Melissa returned the stare with one of her own, which Jenna understood as, *It's not my fault.*

"Blair, what brings you into my shop today? Do you need some monogramming?"

Blair laughed in her snooty aristocratic way and flipped her hair as if posing for nonexistent cameras. Then Jenna looked around, making sure there *were* no cameras. She wouldn't put it past Blair to have someone tailing her, filming her, these days. Some of her recent livestreams were of her doing things around town, usually different activities that there was no way she could film herself.

"A little birdie told me that Melissa's dress was being made in your backroom by none other than Maximilian Thorne. The girl at the cafe was going on and on about how Maximilian Thorne is your uncle. No one ever has seen him in this..." Blair put her nose in the air. "Quaint little town. Now that the holiday magic has worn off, this is just like any other small town, not much to see. I even got caught up in that magic. But I planned on skipping out on coming back. If it hadn't been for my followers nagging me about the wedding, I wouldn't be here."

"Lucky me," Melissa grumbled sarcastically, and Jenna had to cover her laugh with a cough.

"I agree you are lucky that I came."

Goodness, Blair was so full of herself.

She continued, "Any who, it seems the word is spreading that a celebrity is in our midst, and I might add, I am interested too. Talking about it is spicing up my YouTube lives. Views have been a bit of a struggle there these days compared to my TikTok and Instagram."

Jenna and Melissa shared a look that said, *I can't believe she admitted her views are down.*

Blair, oblivious to their silent conversation, kept walking

around looking at the fabrics. She touched a few dropped them quickly, and rubbed her fingers together like the material was dirty. Blair walked closer to Jenna, trying to see behind her into the back room, probably looking for Max. Jenna forgot how pretty she was up close. As pretty as any of the models Jenna worked with on shoots with Max back in the day. She was every girl with self-esteem issues' worst enemy to stand beside. Tall and slender, dressed in expensive jeans, a beautiful silk blouse, and carrying a handbag that probably cost more than Jenna's car.

Jenna said a silent prayer, grateful that Ben wasn't in the shop too. She didn't know how she would take it if he wanted to chase after Blair instead of her. Jenna shivered at the thought. Eventually, Ben would meet her now that she was in town, and it sucked that Jenna could already feel her jealousy rising for no reason. It wasn't like she and Ben were an item, and if Ben was still the same guy he was back in New York, he'd never go for someone as shallow as Blair.

"The girl at the cafe mentioned you showing Maximilian's drawings to Melissa over lunch there. Would you be a dear and go grab them for me to take a quick snapshot to post."

Max came out of the backroom at the worst or possibly the best moment.

"And there he is, the man of the hour." Blair shoved Jenna to the side to get closer to Max. She extended her hand. "Pleasure to meet you. I am Blair Kincaid." And shook his hand. Jenna wondered how she could keep her arm straight with such a large bag that had to weigh a ton. The woman must have forearms of steel.

She snorted at that thought, and Max rolled his eyes at her. Or possibly at Blair, which made her snort again. Everyone looked at her. Melissa covered her laugh in Snickerdoodle's fur. Max tried to keep his lips from turning up in a smile, and Blair looked at her with utter disgust.

"Excuse me, it must be the dust." Jenna faked another cough.

Max was a pro at handling things like this, so Jenna made her way over to Melissa, who was hugging Snickerdoodle so tight she thought she would squash the poor thing.

"I'm so sorry. I had no idea Blair was coming to town today. I am so stupid for letting her invite herself. I swear the minute she arrived, I wished for a brief moment that Jake hadn't proposed to me in front of everyone where she could catch it on video. It's bad enough that it went viral, and I have people contacting me left and right about planning events, but to have her here now is going to be a nightmare. I can't imagine getting everything done that I wanted to surprise Jake with, with her following me around. She will spoil it all by posting it online. I just know it."

"Look, I have an idea. Let me do everything for the surprise party. Then all you have to do is give me a detailed list telling me what to do."

Melissa squealed and gave Jenna a half hug. Snickerdoodle barked in enthusiasm, following her mom's happiness. "You are truly my best friend. I'll send a detailed list over tonight. Now let's go save Max. Blair hasn't stopped taking selfies of them, and he keeps looking my way."

Max was standing in the way of the back room. Jenna could hear Blair practically whining for him to let her see the gown.

"Blair, we won't show you the gown. Melissa wants to surprise Jake, and if it accidentally got online, it would ruin it. I know for a fact that he is a fan and follows you on Instagram."

Blair's feathers seemed to have been stroked. "He does? Well, in that case, I guess I can wait. But my fans will be sadly disappointed."

Max patted Blair on the back. "Just imagine how you can spin this, darling. Pretend you've yourself seen the gown. Everyone will believe it when you post your pictures later. Let them believe you want to keep it a secret for the groom, and your viewers will eat it up."

Blair swatted Max on his arm as if flirting with him as her

boyfriend, Paul, walked into the shop. Paul walked over to Melissa, kissing her on the cheek and greeting her. Blair gave her the evil eye, still jealous that he'd dated Melissa. He then turned to Blair and tapped his watch. "We need to go. Mason called. He convinced the ice rink to open an hour earlier for you to do some filming. Having a lesson with a retired pro will be good for your YouTube channel and you can show off the new outfit from our sponsor."

Blair's demeanor changed now that Paul was around. She became soft and flirty, a little more down to earth, making Jenna wonder which one was her real nature. Blair left Max and walked over to Paul, giving him a full-on hug and kiss. "Wonderful, you are an angel."

Paul grabbed her hand and she waved with her other one. "Ta-ta, see you all bright and early tomorrow morning."

Max whispered out the corner of his mouth, "Poor Melissa."

Jenna nodded in agreement. Blair could definitely be grating.

Melissa crossed the room toward Jenna and Max when the bells chimed on the door again. Blair was back. "Melissa hun, remember to dress..." She moved her forefinger up and down, following the length of Melissa's body. "Better than this when we go to the florist tomorrow. I will be doing a live feed. Can't have you embarrassing my brand, can we?"

She laughed as if she were joking. Blair was about to leave, but instead she paused and pushed the door back open to look back at them. "And wear some makeup, for heaven's sake. We don't want a repeat of you looking like you just woke up, like on your engagement video."

When she left, they all stared at the door in shock, waiting for Blair to come back for one more insult. When it appeared they were spared, Melissa groaned. "I am so dreading tomorrow. Thank goodness Andrea will be coming with me."

"Girls, please excuse me. I will get back to stitching pearls." He bent over to give Melissa a peck on her cheek. "Lovely to see you again, darling, and don't keep this girl too long. We have loads more to do on your dress if you want it ready for the big day."

"I won't stay long." She held up three fingers like a scout. "I promise."

Max chuckled as he walked into the back."

"I'm sorry about the added work of the pearls."

"No worries. Max and I just like to gripe and mess around, don't take us seriously. Plus, it was my idea, and honestly, I love that they were on your mom's dress. It's your 'something old,' and by having them there, it will be like your mom is too."

"Aww, Jenna," Melissa said as Jenna handed her a tissue to wipe her eyes. Melissa handed Snickerdoodle to Jenna and blew her nose. "Dad was thinking the same thing when he found the dress and gave it to me. Actually, if I'm honest, it was Andrea. She had seen a woman on Facebook getting married, and in the segment, the video showed a piece of her mom's dress stitched inside of hers and some parts in the bouquet."

"I saw that video also. It was sweet. It made me cry."

"Me too. To know that I will be able to do the same makes me happy and sad. I wish Mom were here. I know she would be so happy for me. She loved Jake back in high school. It makes me feel good knowing I am marrying a man I know at one point in my life she approved of."

Jenna put Snickerdoodle on the floor and gave Melissa a big hug. They both cried together for a bit. Melissa's mom was like a second mom to her, and she knew how hard it was for Melissa to lose her. Honestly, after her mom died, Melissa's grief was very similar to how Jenna felt when Ben left her. The darkness of loss seemed to seep into every aspect of her life until one day, the drowning sensation slowly lifted, and a pinhole of light started filtering in again. These days, Melissa glowed for the most part, and the sadness that once consumed her seemed to fade.

Melissa even confessed that she and Andrea, the town mayor

and her dad's new wife, had become very close, and she considered her like her mom now.

"I'm so glad Andrea told your dad about that video. She is a wonderful woman," Jenna said.

"She really is. Honestly, some days I feel too old to need a mom, but when I called her Mom for the first time, I think it made her day just as much as it made mine. She told me that I was very much her daughter, and she was grateful to me for thinking of her as a mom. I think when Jake and I have kids, she will spoil them as if they were her very own grandchildren."

"They will be, Mel. Just because she isn't your blood mom, she is very much your mom now and will be very much your kids' grandmother. So don't be ashamed of being lucky enough to have a second mom that you love. It's really a blessing."

"It is, isn't it? Speaking of parents, how is your grandma? Is she recovering from her fall?"

"She ended up having to have her hip replaced. So Mom and Dad will be staying with her until she is out of rehab."

"Will they be back for my wedding, you think?"

"Last I talked to them, they will."

"What about your sister and her family?"

"Leigh Anne is waiting for Daryl to get permission to take military leave. She's so bummed they had to move right when y'all got engaged. She isn't sure if he will get permission, though."

"I totally understand. I bet Daryl is glad to have her and Andrew with him. I can't imagine being in the military and having to be away from my family so much."

"It was hard. She missed him so much and was glad she got to visit him before Christmas and figure out their housing. Oh, I can't believe I forgot to tell you..."

"What?"

"I'm going to be an aunt again."

"Congratulations! I can't wait to start a family with Jake."

"Seriously?"

"Well, I mean not right away, but he will make a great dad."

"Jenna!" Max shouted from the back room, "These pearls won't sew themselves on, and my old hands are done."

"Coming!" she hollered back.

Melissa picked up Snickerdoodle and before she left, she turned back to Jenna. "I'll send the to-do list over to your house tonight around eight."

"You know you don't have to come over to deliver it. You can just send me an email."

Melissa gasped in mock offense. "How dare you insult me and my paper obsession."

"Yeah, yeah, I get it. You might as well stay for a glass of wine tonight when you come. Max will be there."

Melissa said, "Exactly what I was hoping for. Max always brings the good stuff." She left the shop with a chuckle.

CHAPTER TWELVE

*B*en hung up the phone after his weekly check-in with his dad. A month of working in the office without him, his dad now saw why Ben felt the need to sell the building. They just didn't have the staff, the production, or the clients to pay the bills for such a large building, and the sale would get them out of the red and give them enough to put toward Ben's new idea if his dad went for his pitch.

After he talked to Jake about the print-on-demand press and saw the space where Jake planned on having his reception, Ben started to dream of moving to Cypressville. He hoped it would be a big enough sign to Jenna to let her know how serious he was about getting to know her again. Plus, he decided it was time to stop living his dad's dreams and start making his own. With his dad finally coming around to selling the building, he figured that if he had Jenna by his side, he could make the others come to fruition. He would finally open his own bookstore, with its primary focus on supporting local authors. He also would bring his entire office here or let them work remotely if they didn't want to move. He could always hire and train up any local hires to help the small town's economy. His dreams were big, but he couldn't do or say anything about it, especially to his dad, until he talked to Walter.

His phone rang, and an unknown number popped up. His stomach fluttered, wondering if it could be Jenna. "Hello?"

It wasn't Jenna. It was Melissa. "Hey Ben, sorry to call so late."

His fleeting happiness faded.

"It's fine, everything okay?"

"Is Jake with you?"

"No, why?"

"Well, I'm trying to plan a couple of surprises for him and his family before the wedding. His parents are coming back into town in a few days, and their wedding anniversary is coming up. I wanted to have a surprise dinner for them with all their friends. Jake's a blabbermouth, so I was hoping you would help me organize it and keep it secret."

Ben laughed. "So, my man Jake can't keep secrets, good to know. Sure, I'll help."

He could hear Melissa breathe out. "Great, in that case, I left a list of what needs to be done behind the mailbox in the jasmine bush in a large Ziplock bag. I will text you the address where you need to go tonight at eight. Thanks."

Before he could respond, she had already hung up, and a text arrived with an address.

"Well, I guess I'm not only helping her plan, but I'm a delivery boy too."

He arrived at a shotgun-style cottage, painted electric purple with a short black iron fence around the front, at precisely eight o'clock. He opened the gate to a yard that was a gardener's dream. The fragrant scent from all of the flowers was everywhere, and one smelled like patchouli, reminding him of Jenna. He walked up the sidewalk and knocked on one of the smallest front doors he'd ever seen.

When the door opened, Ben was shocked to see the fashion designer from the cafe. The one Jenna hugged and called Max.

Max looked just as surprised to see him as he was to see Max.

"Can I help you?" Max asked.

Ben held the Ziplock with Melissa's papers in it. "Sorry to bother you so late, sir. I'm Ben Sanderson, Jake's best man. Melissa asked me to deliver this here tonight at eight. She hung up before telling me whose house I was going to."

Max put out his hand to shake Ben's. "Maximilian Thorne, but you can call me Max." Ben gave Max the envelope. Max opened the Ziplock and peaked at the papers then closed it up and shoved it back in Ben's hands. "Hmm. Well, I'm not expecting anything from Melissa. It must be for Jenna."

"Jenna? Is she here?"

"This is her house. I'm just visiting."

Ben was shocked, but he shouldn't be. Jenna had warned him that Melissa was trying to play matchmaker.

"Then I guess this is for her. Would you mind giving it to her for me?"

"No, if Melissa sent you here, there must be a reason beyond handing over the papers. Come on in."

Max opened the door wider, and Ben ducked, making sure not to hit his head as he walked into one of the most eclectic houses he'd ever seen. Ben's stomach fluttered in a mix of nerves and excitement seeing Jenna's home. He tried to take in as much as possible to get a feel of twenty-seven-year-old Jenna. Max led him down an incredibly long hall leading to the living room area. Each door he passed was a different color, shape, and style. They were all open, and he couldn't help but glance inside each room as he walked by. They were all different. Each one painted a different vibrant bright color with a mix of modern and antique furniture. The only artwork on the walls was hand-painted pieces of art, not prints. Some looked professional, while others appeared to be done by children if he had to guess.

Strangely, the house fit the Jenna he remembered. Happy, vibrant, and full of life. He could see how a home like hers would make someone feel good just by being inside it. When he reached the kitchen, he expected something just as wild but was surprised when it was all white. White subway tiles, white slate countertop, all the cabinets and the island painted white. Even her bar stools and the cushions were white. The only color he noticed was the hardwood floors.

"You can wait here. Jenna is out back in her garden. I'll go get her."

"Thank you."

Before Max could go outside, Jenna was at the back door swinging it open. Ben thought she looked adorable, her hair in a messy ponytail, dirt smudged on her cheek, beautiful smooth fair-skinned legs, adorned with faded cut off shorts, and a baggy t-shirt. "Good lord, Rocky is back, and he dug up everything I just planted! Adding the spot lights didn't work. I don't know how to keep that darn raccoon out of there without building a greenhouse."

"Jenna," Max said, but she kept rambling as she placed her basket with a few gardening tools on a small table by the back door and started taking off her shoes.

Max said her name louder.

She looked up. "What, Max?" Then her face went beet red when she noticed Ben sitting at her island.

"Ben, what are you doing here?"

Max picked up some keys off the rack by the door. "Darling, I'm going to borrow your car for a bit."

Jenna didn't even look at Max, she kept staring at Ben, but she responded, "Sure."

Ben got up and walked toward her. "I'm sorry to come

unexpectedly. Melissa gave me this to give you. She didn't tell me I was going to your house, though. She hung up too fast, I probably should have figured that out, but I guess I'm slow tonight."

A half-smile crept up on Jenna's face. "That girl is still trying to set us up."

"Well, at least now I know where you live. It's better than last time."

Jenna smiled. "True, true," she said as she opened the large Ziplock.

"By the way, where are you staying?"

"Jake's new house."

"Ooh lucky, I haven't gotten to see it yet. Melissa won't let me until she has it all perfect with her things inside."

"Well, there isn't much to it right now. Jake and I are sleeping on air mattresses and eating on plastic outdoor chairs with TV trays. I think he and Melissa are supposed to go shopping for furniture soon because he mentioned it would be ready for when she moves in after the wedding."

Jenna's brows rose. "Melissa is a little bit of a perfectionist and has to have things her way. I wonder if she will let Jake pick out any furniture."

Ben pulled the papers out of her hand and scanned Melissa's immaculately printed list of names and addresses of the people she wanted to invite. The following section was titled "Chez François." Written below were detailed instructions on how to decorate the back room. He waved the paper. "It appears she is quite organized. I highly doubt Jake will have any input."

Jenna plucked the list back, but Ben's curiosity over the list had him pulling it back to keep reading it.

Then Jenna grabbed it back, laughing. "Hey, this is mine. I'm supposed to be helping her, not you."

"Wrong." He laughed, taking the paper back. "She enlisted my help this evening."

She plucked the paper back with a broad smile. "But she asked for my help first."

Ben grabbed it back and held his hand high in the air. Jenna came at him, they were standing practically chest to chest now, and she jumped up trying to grab it when he tiptoed, making it even higher, laughing now too.

Jenna's breathless laugh ended when she casually placed her hand on his chest to keep balance and grabbed the paper. Her eyes went straight to his. His heart pounded heavily under her palm still resting there. Her face flushed, and her lips looked like they were begging Ben for a kiss. When he heard the paper flutter to the floor and her eyes closed, he took that as his sign that she was more than willing to kiss him back. Ben had his hands around her waist, her head tilted up toward his, he then lifted her off the ground, remembering she loved it when he lifted her to his height. His lips barely brushed hers when the door opened, and Max walked in.

"I forgot my wallet."

Jenna pushed off his chest, ending their moment. He put her down and straightened her t-shirt without thinking. Ben's hands dropped away when he noticed the look of horror cross Jenna's features. She knew Max realized what he'd interrupted and moved farther away from Ben.

Max didn't miss a beat. He nodded to Ben. "Nevermind, I think I left it in the car, carry on." Then he walked back out of the house.

Jenna backed away, clearing her throat. She picked up the dropped paper and cleared her throat again. Finally, she put her finger up telling him to wait, placed the paper on the counter, and ran after Max, but before she got outside, she turned back. "Don't you dare leave."

CHAPTER THIRTEEN

*J*enna ran after Max, afraid that Ben would leave, but the need to go after her uncle trumped her fears of Ben leaving her again. He was walking around the back alley near her garage. "Max! Wait up."

She was out of breath when she reached him.

"Darling, what are you doing chasing me down when you, dear heart, were about to get kissed if it hadn't been for my interruption."

Jenna could feel the heat rise again on her cheeks. She and Melissa always were the easiest people to make blush. She hated it but had honestly forgotten what it felt like. She hadn't had anything to blush over in years.

"Max, I don't want to kiss him."

"Darling, don't fool yourself. You let the man literally sweep you off your feet."

Jenna felt her cheeks get warmer. "Well, it doesn't matter. Those were old residual feelings. I don't even know Ben anymore. Too many years have passed. You of all people should understand."

Max patted her cheek. "I do understand, but there are some

occasions that rise up, and we need to take the leap of faith that will align things again. I don't want you to miss out because you're afraid."

"I'm not afraid." Jenna fisted her hands hanging at her sides and stomped her foot in indignation. "I just want to get to know this Ben before I go kissing him and getting all confused in my feelings."

"As long as you understand that, darling, that is all that matters. I just wanted to make sure you didn't build up your walls again."

"Forget about me and my walls. You don't have to leave. Ben and I are going to go over Melissa's list for the surprise she is planning for Jake. It's not like Ben came here for me anyway. He came because Melissa enlisted his help too, and now I'm enlisting you."

"You sure?"

"Yes. Come on."

Max and Jenna returned to the house and Ben was right where she left him. Relief swept through her like an ocean wave. Max glanced at her from the corner of his eye with a smirk playing around his lips. She knocked his arm with her elbow, whispering "shut up." But Max's smile grew bigger.

Jenna watched Ben watch her and Max. He squinted his eyes in that adorably perplexed way that nearly made them disappear. When he finally spoke, he asked, "Did I miss something?"

Jenna shoved Max to the side a bit and stood in front of him. "No! You missed absolutely nothing." Then she jumped up to sit on her countertop. "Now, hand me the list Melissa sent us, and let's figure out what she wants us all to do. Max, would you please make some coffee? I'm sure we will be here for a while to figure out what each of us will be taking on."

Ben turned to Max. "I don't need any coffee, thanks. Actually, Jenna, there isn't much really for us to do."

Jenna took the paper out of Ben's hand when he brought it

over to her. She looked at the page, and he was right. The details were all there, but it said it was a project for her and Ben to do together. They were in charge of decorating the restaurant, and the list had a diagram of the room and precisely what each decoration looked like and where it went. The other part was an address list that had her and Ben going in person to invite all Jake's parents' friends and to explain it was a surprise fortieth wedding anniversary party.

"I don't get it. Why do we have to do this together? It would be so much simpler if we split the list three ways and went to invite everyone."

Max handed Jenna a cup of coffee and pulled the list from Jenna's free hand. "Aha, it says right here in all caps 'Don't ask for any help outside of Ben.'"

Max laughed and put the paper down. "I guess I'm out. I'll be going to bed now. Goodnight."

"Max, it's not even nine," Jenna shouted at the retreating form.

Max waved away her statement without even turning around, and Ben was no help at all as he told Max goodnight.

What was she supposed to do now? Ben was in her house, her space, her safe haven. A place she created to forget him, and now he was invading it. What if he left again? Would she have to move again to forget him?

"Okay, well, I guess you need to head out." She jumped down from the counter and was practically bouncing on her toes, itching to get rid of Ben. She didn't want to see him all over her house. She started pushing him toward the front door.

"I get it. You don't have to push me. You want me gone." He sounded aggravated yet still laughed.

She couldn't care about his feelings. She had to build up her barriers until she knew him better. "Look, Max is right. It's late. Why don't you meet me at Main Street Java tomorrow around ten, and we can sort out Melissa's list." She glanced at the list, then back at Ben standing in the doorway of her front door.

Wow, she forgot how tall he was until he was standing next to her smaller-than-average door. His head was over the six-foot molding at the top of the sixteenth-century door she found at an antique auction years ago. Of course, she was only five-four, so the doorway was always big enough for her, and Max was only probably five-nine or ten. But, my goodness, how had she never paid attention to how low he had to bend down for their kisses? Maybe because he'd always lifted her up to his height. She loved when he did that. It made her feel so much more of his energy merging with hers, being in his arms that close. Their connection was always so intense.

He turned his head and looked up at the head jamb. "Why is your door so small?"

"I found it at an auction and fell in love with the old-time feel; felt like it would suit my house."

Ben chuckled, he noticed earlier that all the doors in the house were different shapes and sizes, but the front door was the smallest. "It does, Jenna. Your house suits you. It's very vibrant, whimsical, and full of surprises, just like you."

Her eyes went straight to his mouth, watching his smooth lips move gracefully over his teeth while he spoke. He licked his lips, which were now glossy, begging to be kissed. They started moving again, but she couldn't seem to concentrate and make out what he was saying. Jenna attempted to shake her head to clear it and stop it from progressing to carnal thoughts. Her voice came out higher than usual, "The party is in two days, so we need to get started. Is tomorrow good?"

He gave her his squinty look again then smiled. "You didn't hear a word I said, did you?"

She felt her cheeks heat up again and placed her hands on them to cool them. "Ben," she whined, "don't make fun of me."

"I wasn't making fun. I was making a statement."

"Still, I swear I haven't blushed this much in years, but being around you is making me incredibly nervous and embarrassed. This is hard." Jenna flung her hand over her mouth.

Ben placed his hand on her shoulder. "I get it. I'm sorry this is so awkward. I feel it too. The old connection is still there for me because I never really let it go. I promise I won't try and kiss you again. It was inappropriate of me, especially since we are technically supposed to be strangers. Does Max know about me?"

Jenna felt as if a giant bucket of cold water had fallen on her. He didn't want to kiss her. It was just the past creeping in. Her heart ached at that knowledge. Why was her mind so stupid, wanting him to want her but not wanting him to want her? She made no sense and struggled with her heart. But he was right. She wanted to act like strangers, and he needed to know who to act in front of. "Max doesn't know much, but he figured out the reason I came home years ago was because of heartache. He said he recognized it back then, and when Max saw my reaction to you at the cafe, he figured you were the one. Only a past love would ever get a reaction like that out of a Thorne, he had told me."

"So can I be normal in front of him when we three are together?"

"Sure, I guess if Max and Walter make up, you can talk to Walter, but if you do, please tell Walter to keep it on the down-low. He is just as much a blabbermouth as I am, and I cannot afford to have Melissa find out. She was devastated when her dad kept his engagement a secret for a few weeks before figuring out how to tell her, and she ended up finding out from Walter."

Ben whistled. "Jake told me she had some minor trust issues, but dang, that's harsh. Are you sure you don't want to tell her? It would make this all so much easier."

"Absolutely not! She would be devastated. We have to keep pretending, and don't you dare tell Jake because he will not keep secrets from her ever."

"I won't, but I still think this is wrong."

"Think whatever you want, but you promised to play along."

"Yeah, yeah," Ben said, unenthused, as he turned around to walk down the sidewalk to the front of her house where he parked on the road. When he got to the car, he turned back to her and waved. "See you tomorrow at ten."

From her front door, she waved, upset, because deep down she wished he would have insisted on staying.

CHAPTER FOURTEEN

*B*en woke up before sunrise, excited about seeing Jenna again today. At least now he knew for sure that seeing each other was affecting her as much as him. She practically admitted he made her nervous, and she was definitely going to let him kiss her.

He stood at the base of the stairs in Jake's den, daydreaming about what it would have felt like to have her willingly in his arms again. All he could hope was that her nervousness was a good sign, that she missed him as much as he missed her. Now to figure out how to prolong their time together. Too bad the surprise party for Jake's folks was in a couple of days. Maybe he'd have to figure out how to volunteer them to help Melissa with more of her wedding plans.

He chuckled to himself. Never in a million years did he think he'd find Jenna. Hopefully, Melissa will keep up her matchmaking because he won't let Jenna go so easily this time. Now that he knew where she lived, it didn't matter if the woman ever gave him her phone number. Melissa gave him the greatest gift in his life, the knowledge of where to find Jenna.

His affinity for Melissa grew because of her effort to play

matchmaker. If it were any other person besides Jenna, he probably would be annoyed, but Melissa knew her best friend well enough to know she would be perfect for him. How unbelievably coincidental.

"Morning, Ben, you're up early."

"Yeah, I couldn't sleep, so I figured I'd get some work in. I got a call yesterday that we had a bite on purchasing the building."

"That was fast." Jake got up from the couch and walked to the kitchen to make some coffee for the the two of them.

Ben followed. "I know. I could see the sadness in my dad's eyes over the phone. I don't think he's ready for this."

"Maybe not, but doesn't he see the benefits in reopening the press but in on-demand form? This will bring back his original dream, only modernized."

"I know that, you know that, and I think he logically knows that, but after leaving the military and having to find a new career and building it up, that building became a symbol of his rebirth. Or at least that's what Mom tells me."

Jake sat at his counter with his coffee. "That honestly makes sense. I know that when we grieve the loss of something, like when Molly passed away in the car accident or, in your dad's case, forced retirement from the military, we tend to latch on to other things to keep us going. I did it with work and not coming home. You, with the girl you loved in college. I think you, like me, latched on to work but I also think you haven't lost hope of finding her again."

Ben shifted uncomfortably. "I don't know about that."

"What a joke. You worked harder than I did. You lived and breathed work and never took a day off until recently. Correct me if I'm wrong, but weren't you working the first day I saw you in town? You seemed like you were still working when you were supposed to be relaxing."

"Well, I was working, but I've slowed down some."

Jake took a sip of his coffee, watching Ben above the rim. "You know, you do seem way more relaxed lately." Then his brows lifted, and his eyes widened. "Holy smokes, Melissa was right!"

Ben nervously glanced at Jake. "What are you on about?"

"You like Jenna!"

Ben was flabbergasted. "What! How in the world did you get something like that out of our conversation about selling our building?"

"It's just that you are relaxed. You slowed down, and you've often disappeared for hours at a time to go into town. You practically live at Main Street Java. We've told you that Jenna goes often, Melissa has even hinted at the times Jenna goes and you always are there during those times. You're trying to run into her accidentally." Jake laughed and slapped his hand on his knee when Ben struggled to find a comeback.

Jake continued, "You might as well admit it. I can see it written all over your face. Lissy will be over-the-moon happy. She told me Jenna would help you get over your college love, but I didn't believe her."

"Wait, what? She knows?"

"Yeah, sorry, man, it was one night when I woke up in the middle of the night in the hospital. My fever finally broke and I was breathing better. Lissy and I started talking about love, and somehow our friends came up. We were both being sentimental, hoping you both would find lasting love. And somehow, we got on the topic of you and Jenna never going on dates. Lissy thinks that something happened when Jenna was in New York, something that hurt her so badly she wants to pretend it never happened, but when she and I were getting to know one another again last Christmas, she and Jenna argued about love. Lissy tends to dwell on things, and she told Jenna off after thinking about what Jenna said. She thinks Jenna was in love, but something bad must have happened. We think Jenna latched on to home improvement as a way to cope. Wait until you see her house."

Ben rushed to look at his phone to hide his expression. He couldn't let Jake know he'd already seen Jenna's house. He muttered, "What about her house?"

"It is a rainbow of colors. The outside is a garish purple, but most of the neighbors have slowly started painting theirs bright colors over the years. Not as bright as Jenna's, but definitely bright. Now the street reminds me of some of the homes in the French Quarter in New Orleans."

Ben had thought the same thing. "What's the big deal about her house being bright?" He glanced at Jake.

Jake sat up then leaned forward, resting his elbow on his knees. His voice lowered, and Ben found himself imitating Jake. "If Jenna knew I told you this, she'd probably throw a shoe at my head."

Ben chuckled. "It can't be that bad." But, deep in the pit of his stomach, he knew it was somehow going to be awful and more than likely his fault.

"That house was originally Jenna's uncle's house. Jenna took it over when she moved back home from New York. Her parents practically forced her to get a job and move out because she was depressed and didn't do anything for months. Lissy told her she should try and paint the house to give her something to do. It was after Lissy came back home after graduation that she saw the entire house completed, and Jenna confessed that how colorful it was helped ease her depression."

Ben sat up straight and rubbed the ache in his chest. Discovering how bad Jenna had been made him sick. "How is Jenna now?"

"Jenna is Jenna. She is truly an amazing girl. She is full of spirit and still bubbly on the outside, but when she thinks no one is looking, we can all see she is still hiding her sadness. We've tried so many things to get her to talk about it, but if there is one thing we learned, we need to let her be. But someone in this town is always watching to make sure she is okay. Everyone feeds her gossip because if she is chatting away, hopefully, she won't ever be alone during her hard times."

"What? Is it like seasonal depression? You know that I've been taking Prozac for years. Has anyone ever mentioned for her to see a professional or even a therapist? Maybe talking to a stranger would help her."

Living with his desertion all these years and never telling a soul must have been soul-crushing. Even though he never let her go, talking about her helped him not live a life of total desperation.

Jake smacked his hand on his knee, jolting Ben out of his thoughts. "I think you may be on to something. You could say it's seasonal. I only just learned of it when I was in the hospital talking to Lissy for hours. But she told me that Jenna is at her worst in the spring and she was worried when Jenna started having a hard time again now that the wedding was so near. She thinks Jenna might be struggling a bit watching us be so happy."

Jake must have confused Ben's expression for confusion, which was a good thing because Ben couldn't let him know that Jenna most assuredly was having a bad spell, not because of them but because he was back in her life, opening up old wounds.

If only he could leave and let her go back to her life. Maybe now that she knows he didn't want to leave on purpose, she can heal. He felt his dreams of being with her slowly drifting away.

But he couldn't leave, and he still had to see Jenna. They had to work together because Melissa and Jake needed their help, and right now they were more important. But if he was going to be seeing Jenna this morning, he had to have more facts. Melissa knew Jenna best these days, and Ben wanted to pick Jake's brain more but didn't quite know what to ask first without looking guilty of hiding his own secrets.

Ben asked, "So, did Jenna's colorful house end up helping her, or is she still as bad off as she was eight years ago?"

"Yeah, Jenna is much better today. As I said, she has her

moments, according to Lissy, but overall, she is good. I don't want you to get the wrong idea about her."

"I'm not. I'm kinda relieved knowing she has healed from her past."

"I wouldn't go that far." Jake chuckled. "This kind of leads into me telling Lissy all about you and the girlfriend you lost."

Ben groaned. He was ready to leave and hibernate, lick his wounds well enough to be able to handle seeing Jenna that morning. "What did you tell her?"

Jake stood up, and on the way to refill his coffee, he patted Ben on the shoulder. "Only that you are the most wanted bachelor in the metropolitan area, and you haven't dated anyone in all the years that I've known you because you are still waiting for Cinderella to show up to the ball. Only you lost the glass slipper."

"Jake, that is ridiculous and not precisely true. I have gone on dates."

Jake laughed, "Okay, that was corny. I've been playing dolls with Megan too much lately. But you're wrong, you may have gone to dinner, but you haven't had a relationship."

Ben stood by the island across from Jake, who took a sip of his coffee.

"Anyway, after Lissy heard your story and got to know you, she deemed you were perfect for Jenna, and only you would be able to bring her out of her dating slump. Don't give me the evil eye. Lissy is a hopeless romantic. Be grateful I didn't do as she wanted, or you would have been introduced earlier. She has been pressuring me to set y'all up on a date since just after I got out of the hospital."

Ben's heart raced. He could have met her sooner. He wished Jake would have attempted to set them up, so much time was wasted. He loosened his collar with his finger, nearly suffocating all of a sudden, trying to keep the truth from Jake. If only Jenna knew how hard it was for him to keep this in. He loved her, he always loved her, and he knew he would never not love her. His mom had always told him that you can be with anyone and make a relationship work, but the universe has chosen one person that you will mesh with so easily it was as if your souls were connected at birth. When you find that person, no one else will ever compare, so hold them close. His mom knew that Jenna was that person for him, and she always kept a candle lit as a prayer that he'd find her again one day.

No matter how much he wanted to tell Jake how right Melissa was about him and Jenna being perfect for one another, he couldn't. There was no way he'd betray Jenna's trust. She needed to get to know him again, and it didn't matter that Melissa thought they would get along. He needed to prove to Jenna that he wasn't that different from the man she fell in love with all those years ago.

CHAPTER FIFTEEN

*B*en seemed so odd this morning. He kept looking at her with sad eyes, and it was beginning to make Jenna uncomfortable. By the time they reached the fifth house, she'd had enough. His energy was rubbing off on her, and she almost burst into tears. She stopped on the sidewalk in front of the Brasseaux's house and pulled Ben's upper arm back to stop him.

Ben turned to Jenna. "Everything okay?"

"No, Ben, it's not."

His sad eyes became concerned as he started to shift from one foot to another. His hands kept lifting like he wanted to grab her hands, or he'd step forward as if he were going to hug her, then he'd stop himself. He was acting so strangely. She knew that last night was awkward with the almost-kiss, but she never remembered Ben being this odd. Well, she took that thought back. He was a nervous wreck who could barely get two words out when they first met. She found herself chuckling at that memory.

Poor Ben looked even more confused now.

"Jenna, I—" he started and shut his mouth, rubbed his hand in his hair, then tried again, "I'm—" and he stopped again and turned around as if to start walking to the Brassseaux's house.

"Ben, stop."

He did but didn't turn around, so Jenna went to him. She stood right in front of him, got on her tiptoes, and placed her hands on his shoulders. Ben turned his head away from her like an upset child. "Ben, look at me."

He turned his eyes to her. She could have sworn he had tears in them.

"What is going on with you today? You are acting stranger than usual. I mean, I know last night was a bit awkward, but I can move past it. I want to get to know you again, not act like strangers to this extent where you can't even say two words to me."

He breathed out, and a tear slipped down his cheek. She couldn't handle him being so sad and hugged him. He squeezed her tightly and placed his cheek on top of her head. Oh, how she missed this. Ben mumbled into her hair. "I'm sorry, Jenna, so very sorry."

She didn't know if he was apologizing for last night or for the past once again, and all she could do was squeeze him a little tighter.

It wasn't until Walter walked out of his house a few doors down and was practically right next to them before she remembered they were out in the open and anyone could see that she and Ben were hugging, and she panicked.

"Hello, kids," Walter said in passing.

Jenna broke away from Ben as if she were on fire. She felt her cheeks heat up and knew they were bright red. "Walter, you're out of your house!"

"That I am, figured I hid long enough. I should take notes from you two. It seems you've mended your past miscommunications."

Jenna turned to Ben, who gave her a small smile, then back to Walter. "You could say that."

Ben grabbed her hand and squeezed it. Was that what he was

hoping for? Was that why he was upset? Because he thought she didn't want to get to know him again? Jenna's mind was spinning.

"That is good to see. It gives me some hope. Jenna, sugar, do you know where I can find Max today? I think he and I have some catching up to do."

Jenna's smile broadened so wide she thought her cheeks would split. "He is at my house. You are one-hundred percent welcome to just walk right in and surprise him."

Walter gave Jenna a peck on the cheek and clapped Ben on the shoulder. "Be good, you two."

Jenna watched Walter walk away with a bounce to his step and squealed in glee. "This makes me so happy."

She pulled out her phone and called him on FaceTime. In her excitement, she bounced up and down. She practically screamed out, "Max!" When he answered the phone.

"Someone sounds happy, is your date going well?" Max smiled at the other end.

Ben leaned into the video. "I hope so." He smiled into the phone as Jenna shooed him back.

"Max, I wanted to prepare you."

"Prepare me for what?" He had the phone close to his eyes as if he were trying to see her better.

"You are about to have a visitor. You better go gussy up, don't want to be caught in your loungers."

"Who's coming over?"

"Someone you've been worrying about over the past few weeks."

Max's phone fell to the floor. She and Ben watched as he fumbled with it. "He's coming here? Now?"

"Yes." Jenna smiled as she still bounced in excitement. "I knew he would forgive you. Walter is the kindest man I know, and if he is ready to forgive, I know y'all will get back together. It's destiny, and he can't do better than you."

"Darling, you are only saying that because you love me."

"I'm saying it because it's true. Now go get ready." She hung up the phone before Max could say anything else.

Ben grabbed her hand again. "So, do we get a second chance too?"

Jenna lifted her eyes to him. Her happiness over Max and Walter made her admit her feelings. She deserved a second chance as well, and it seemed that's what Ben wanted too.

Her heart pounded in her ears, love overflowed in her heart. She gripped his hand tight in hers. "Yes. I'd really like that."

Ben whooped and lifted her, spinning her around. "Thank you, Jenna! You've made me the happiest man alive."

Jenna laughed as the lightness inside of her spread throughout her entire being. She hadn't been this genuinely happy in ages.

Ben set her down, and hand in hand they walked to the Brasseaux's house to invite them to the anniversary party for Jake's parents that weekend.

CHAPTER SIXTEEN

he last few days had flown by as Jenna and Ben became friends again. They spent practically every minute together each day, and Jenna talked Ben into helping her weed her garden. He readily agreed and was surprisingly good with the plants, especially since he said he had never gardened before. Their conversations flowed easily, and the tension of being together again lessened with each visit.

Jenna sat back on her heels on the row of vegetables across from Ben and watched him work. He had a smudge of dirt on his sun-pinkened cheek. He caught her staring and smiled so wide his top lip thinned, showing all his teeth. She couldn't help smiling back as her heart swelled in happiness. She hurried to start weeding again, slightly embarrassed. She heard Ben chuckle, but when she peeked up at him, he was back at work.

She was amazed at how easy spending time with Ben was and that she could envision them doing this all the time. Suddenly her stomach dropped, and her heart started racing. She swallowed hard as her mouth went dry with the realization that she was in love with Ben again.

Jenna started pulling weeds as if her entire life depended on it, trying to wipe away the romanticized images that were popping into her mind. She couldn't fall this fast for him. It terrified her. What if he leaves again? Surely, he won't stay. He had a life, living hours away. They would have to have a long-distance relationship. But that wouldn't work, and she didn't want to move.

Part of her fears about being successful as a fashion designer was that she'd have to move. She loved Cypressville. It's where she grew up and where she healed when she came back home. The town, the people, were all like family, and she needed them. They were what kept her sane. Ben would have to move here, but she knew that he and his dad owned a publishing company.

She and Ben seemed to automatically resume their relationship following the same rules she set up in the past. No talk about their current lives and family other than just the basics. What was her issue with playing games with him? He was more than likely sick of them. Look what it cost them, eight years apart and him going to therapy because of his guilt. At least she'd fared better than him, which upset her because she didn't deserve it. She wished he would just move here and make her life easier.

She groaned at herself, upset for thinking so selfishly and for constantly reverting back to her twenty-year-old self when near him. She wished she could figure out why she could be so clearheaded with everyone else except with Ben. "Jenna." Ben broke her concentration.

Before she knew it, she'd thrown the weeds in her hand at his face.

He laughed good-naturedly. Guilty at taking her anger and her frustrations out on him, Jenna hurriedly apologized. "Sorry, I was in a zone."

"You were pulling those weeds out with some serious energy." He wiped off some strands of discarded weeds from his shoulder.

Exasperated, Jenna had to come up with some excuse for her behavior. When she noticed how pink Ben's neck was, she used the afternoon sun as her out. "I think the heat is getting to me." She sat back and wiped her gloved hands against one another, and looked at her watch. "Anyway, it's already two o'clock. We only have a few hours to clean up before the Blessings' anniversary party, and I promised Melissa I would go early to help her rearrange any of the decorations that you and I set up last night that aren't right."

"Wow, is it that late already?" Ben jumped up quickly, stepped over the row of vegetables she just weeded, and held his hand to her. Jenna took his offered hand and out of the blue, the thought of them being together again scared her. How would their relationship work? She still didn't have his phone number and couldn't understand why she was so stubborn in not giving hers to him. Seriously, he knew where she lived, what was the big deal in giving him her number? For some reason she just couldn't make herself give in.

Jenna turned away from him, letting go of his hand, not wanting to give her feelings away, but Ben grabbed her hand again, pulling her back. She stumbled a bit and he caught her, bringing her close. Jenna couldn't think when she was this close to him. All she wanted him to do was tilt down and kiss her. Hurriedly, she stepped back. She couldn't go there.

Ben noticed, his beautiful smile disappeared, and a blank neutral expression took over. Her chest ached at the thought of hurting him.

He put his hands in the pockets of his shorts and started rocking on his heels. He looked nervous.

"Did you want to ask me something?"

"Well, I was wondering if we could go together tonight. I can pick you up at six if you'd like?"

She was grateful for the timing of the kids running across the back alleyway, screaming in childish joy, making Ben turn his head. It gave her time to take a deep breath and control the excitement and fear of accepting. For some reason, this felt like a turning point. She knew she couldn't keep playing games, and Jenna decided that if she accepted, she'd stop. He deserved better, and this time they would talk about a possible future. It both excited and scared her at the same time. By the time he turned his attention back to her, he was smiling.

Ben had always loved kids, and that was one of the things that drew her to him. She wanted a big family one day. Jenna loved her family, even though it had been hard to babysit her baby nephew, Andrew, for a week last year at Christmas, and she may have complained that she wasn't ready. But once her sister got back and they moved to be with her brother-in-law Daryl, she missed him dreadfully and knew if she had her own child, she would be excessively happy.

Jenna graced Ben with a huge smile in return. "I'd love that."

Within seconds Ben embraced her. The scent of the earth and the warmth of the sun on his clothes and skin drew her in and made her hug him tighter. She would not take any moment with him for granted now. She wouldn't obsess about the future. Instead, she would just embrace the love.

CHAPTER SEVENTEEN

*B*en and Jenna arrived to the restaurant to only one car in the parking lot. Jenna turned to Ben, "I wonder if Melissa's dad dropped her off?"

Ben shrugged his shoulders in response. He got to the door first he attempted to open it for Jenna, but found it was locked.

Jenna turned to Ben, "That's weird."

Ben knocked on the door.

It took a minute before a flustered François greeted them with a hug and a kiss on both cheeks.

"Bonjour, Jenna, Ben." François started looking around them. He was red-cheeked and seemed on the verge of a nervous breakdown. "Where is Melissa? She was supposed to set the place settings. Mon sous-chef est malade."

Jenna gave him a questioning look.

François transitioned to English: "Sick, two wait staff quit, and I am not able to help her as I anticipated. I need to get the food prepared."

"She isn't here?"

François looked at her as if she were stupid. She hurriedly

pulled out her phone and called Melissa. "Where are you?" Jenna asked when Melissa answered.

She listened to Melissa for a few seconds. Then turned to the men. "Jake held her up at home, and she was late picking up the cake. She's on her way now."

François made a hand gesture, muttering something in French that made Ben snicker. François gave him a side glare. "You two will have to do, non?"

They walked in, following the chef as he rushed to the kitchen. He pulled out a rolling cart loaded down with plate chargers, silverware, cloth napkins, and a seating chart.

As he rushed off to the stove and Ben and Jenna didn't move quick enough, he shouted, "Get to work!"

Ben turned to Jenna, trying not to laugh. "I guess it's up to us to finish setting things up. I hope Melissa's instructions for the place setting are in as much detail as the decorations that we had to do."

"I'm sure it will be."

Jenna yelped when Ben passed her with a wicked grin as he pushed the cart and nudged her with his elbow making her off balance. "Get to work," he said and sped walked away.

"Hey now, none of that!" she shouted back at him.

They both joked and laughed while setting the tables until Jenna decided Ben needed a little payback while his back was turned. She opened one of the cloth napkins, grabbed two corners between her fingers, spun it until it was tightly wound, then swatted Ben on the rear end with it.

The towel made a loud snap when it hit his butt. Ben yelped, dropped the fork he was holding, and rubbed the sore spot. Jenna, shocked at the impact, put her hands over her mouth and started laughing.

Ben pulled a napkin undone and started to get it ready for his retribution.

"Oh no, you don't." Jenna laughed as she moved behind a

chair, using it as her first line of defense. Then, when Ben shifted right, she turned left. Both laughed when he finally swatted it and missed her by an inch.

Before he was done spinning his again, she had hers twisted and whacked him again. Ben laughed as he rubbed his hip this time.

Ben said, "Umma is going to be happy to know she finally has some good competition."

Jenna stopped laughing, breathing heavily at Ben's words. Did that mean he wanted her to meet his mom? Before she could dwell on it any longer, they both heard François' rapid-fire speech, half in French and half in English. When they heard Melissa apologizing, they made their way to the front of the restaurant. Melissa was carrying a large cake box and looking a little flustered herself. François walked to the kitchen and returned with a cake stand, muttering something about a wasted Galette des Rois.

Melissa gave him an apologetic half-smile, "It won't be wasted. I ordered it because it's Mrs. Blessing's favorite dessert."

Ben took that as his signal to hurry to Melissa's side and take the heavy cake from her hands. She grabbed the cake stand from François and kissed him on his cheek, thanking him for his help. He patted her on the cheek and went back to his kitchen. Melissa walked to the back room where they had decorated. "Wow, you guys followed my directions to a T. I may have to hire you both if I ever decide to expand."

Ben placed the cake on the desert table and Melissa took the cake out of the box and placed it on the stand. Then, she pulled out a small bag from her tote on the floor and started decorating it with a few spring flowers. Once done, she started walking around the room and moving things a tiny bit here and there. "Seriously, you guys did great."

Jenna beamed. "It was fun." She elbowed Ben in the ribs.

"It sure was."

Melissa chuckled at them. "Well, if either of you ever changes your mind about your careers and needs a job. I'm always looking for someone who follows the details."

Ben laughed at that. "I may take you up on that. I've never seen anyone as detailed as you."

Jenna's heart started to pump with excitement at the prospect of Ben's words. She had to calm herself down, telling herself he didn't mean it for real.

Ben continued talking to Melissa, not noticing the skip in the beat of her chest and the disappointment that followed after his next words. "Melissa, if you are anywhere near as talented in book organization, I may need to have you come work for me instead and get my office in order." They both laughed.

Jenna grabbed the empty cake box and took it to the kitchen. She had to take a moment to breathe. For a moment, she thought she was going to cry. This was so hard, hiding her true feelings from not only Ben but Melissa too. She'd see right through Jenna and know something was up and tonight wasn't the night to go into deep conversations. She had to grow up soon, and Ben was right. It wasn't good of her to hide one of the best memories of her life from her best friend. She should have told Mel a long time ago about Ben.

She took a deep breath, found her bottle of water in her purse at the rack near the room's entrance, and took a sip before rejoining Melissa and Ben to finish putting everything together.

CHAPTER EIGHTEEN

*B*en hadn't been able to take his eyes off of Jenna since the moment he picked her up that evening. She had to be the most beautiful woman he'd ever seen. She had her hair twisted up and her bangs pushed to the side, showing off her full dark brows. She reminded him of a 1950s actress in her full white skirt and fitted top. She skipped down her front steps in her hot pink heels as he opened the garden gate.

"Jenna, you look stunning."

She spun around twice for him, making her skirt spin. "I love this design and have been dying for an occasion to wear it." She lifted the bottom of the skirt. "See, it has multiple layers of color, so when you spin or dance, you will get little peeks of them."

"Well, I guess that means we will be dancing the night away, showing off all your colors."

Jenna laughed, placing her hand over his heart. "You better believe it. I missed dancing with you. I've never found a partner with near as much flair."

Ben chortled at that. "What, you missed my two left feet?"

She laughed. "You, Ben, never had two left feet. Don't be so modest. I missed how when you get on the dance floor, all that cool reserve melts away and you become a wild child."

Ben took her hand and did a few dance moves while twirling her around and around. Jenna laughed heartily when, dizzy, she grabbed both his arms.

Ben held her close, swaying with her on her sidewalk. "So, you missed my one-and-only impressive dance move, huh?"

She nodded then pushed off his chest. "We better hurry, or we'll be late."

They weren't late but it wasn't long before Jake, his parents, Susan, and Megan arrived and everyone shouted "Surprise!"

Jenna greeted them all as if they were extended family and introduced Ben to them as Jake's boss and best man. To say he was disappointed was a given, but he shouldn't have been, knowing good and well that she wasn't about to let anyone know they were seeing each other again. Or that they ever dated to begin with. He wished she would be honest with everyone, especially since the last few days they'd been practically attached at the hip, and he loved every moment of it.

He wanted forever with Jenna, but if she kept changing the topic every time he tried to talk about his family, his future at work, or her family and job, he wasn't sure it would work. It's like she had grown up and stayed young all at the same time. When they were themselves without talking about anything major, he fell more and more in love with her. His feelings for her, he discovered, hadn't changed. They got along, in his opinion, easier and better than they did years ago, probably because he didn't get nearly as tongue-tied by her as he did back in college.

He watched her talking to Susan and Mr. and Mrs. Blessing for a while, then turned to the opposite side of the room where Max and Walter stood. Both were wearing Max's designs. Max wore a monochromatic lavender suit and Walter had on a pale blue suit and the same color shirt as Max. When they caught eyes across the room, the two men walked over to Ben.

Walter patted Ben on the back. "I see a man with love written all over his face. What about you, Max? Do you see it too?"

Ben adjusted his tie and Max gave Ben an assessing look. Then his eyes lit up in recognition that it was one of his own designs. With a huge smile on his face, he said, "I'd say you're right, Walt. So, darling, what are we going to do about this? Should we give him the interrogation?"

Ben said sarcastically, "You two are too funny," then turned the topic around onto them. "It appears you've made up?"

Walter turned to Max, and Max placed his arm around Walter's shoulders. "That we did. It was a long time coming, and we've had several long nights of conversations."

"Full of tears, hollering, and forgiveness," Walter interjected.

"That we did."

Ben, normally never one to be nosy, had to ask. "If you don't mind me prying, how do you plan to make the relationship work long distance?"

Walter was about to readily answer before Max squeezed his shoulder, hushing his response. Walter gave Ben a sympathetic look.

"It's alright," Ben said. "I know it's none of my business."

Max gave Ben a stern look. "Jenna is like a granddaughter to me. I love that child more than anything, and you hurt her terribly in the past."

Ben opened his mouth to say something, and Walter stepped out from under Max's arm and gave him a severe look. Before Ben could get his words out, Max grabbed Walter's hand and held it tight as he spoke. "Since Jenna's father is still away, I feel it's only my duty to see what your intentions are for my grand-niece before I tell you about Walter and me."

Ben didn't have to think about it. He had enjoyed spending the last few days with Jenna. He knew that the chemistry they still had was there. Although she was more reserved, the effect of her nearness and conversations still gave him that same spark of happiness from his youth. Her entire energy melded with his. But could he hope for anything more with her? Deep down, he knew that he wanted to be with her forever. Even though she still played the game, he had decided that he still wanted to be with her, he wouldn't let her go this time.

He knew he had to talk to his dad. Ben knew Jenna well enough to know she wasn't going to move. It would be up to him. After his dad had been at the office for this last two months, he'd seen for himself the decline of the publishing industry for small companies like theirs. EBooks were taking over, and they needed to make changes. Joon had worn Jonathan down while Ben was away, and his dad had agreed to retire. After several video calls, he decided to sell the building and agreed to the new print on demand and having the employees work from home. They could come to the office once a week when they found a new space. Now he needed to convince his dad Cypressville was the location for that.

Ben noticed Max's lips curve up in a smile. "I see those wheels turning, clearly you're starting to figure it out."

Ben returned his grin. "You are a wise man, Max. I am."

Max turned to Walter and kissed his cheek, then held his hand out to Ben. Ben shook it as Max pulled him into a hug and whispered in his ear, "I decided to retire and move back home, and from the look on your face, I think you have come to a similar conclusion."

Ben caught Jenna's eyes across the room, and her perfectly shaped brow quirked. All he did was wink and smile in response. Within seconds she was headed his way.

"What in the world was all that about with you and Max?"

Ben pulled her onto the dance floor and spun her around. Jenna's skirt flared, and she smiled happily when she returned to his arms. As they swayed Ben caught a glance of Mr. and Mrs.

Blessing, and Melissa and Jake dancing near them, smiling at them. Jake winked at him and mouthed, "You like her" and Ben nodded.

Seconds later, Melissa squealed in glee. He pulled Jenna close.

"Something has made you terribly happy," Jenna said.

"You, Jenna. You've made me happy."

CHAPTER NINETEEN

*W*ith only a few days until Melissa's wedding, she stood on a small pedestal wearing her gown for the final fitting. Jenna turned her to the mirror. Melissa put her hands to her mouth and cried. "It's beautiful. I'm beautiful."

"You've always been beautiful, you silly girl."

Melissa rubbed her hand gently down the front of her bodice. "Is this center section a part of my mom's gown too?"

"Yes, Max and I figured out a way to add it at the last minute."

"Jenna," Melissa breathed out, and with weepy eyes choked out, "Thank you."

Jenna grabbed a few tissues and handed them to Melissa, and wiped her own eyes in the process. "Dry those eyes. The silk won't look so good if it has tear stains running all down the front."

Melissa wiped her eyes and spun around, looking at herself in the mirror. "I can't believe that in just a few days, I'll be married! I will be Mrs. Jake Blessing."

"Girl! I'm so excited for you. I swear you've been dreaming of this day since you were sixteen."

"I know, right?" The joy in Melissa's voice filled Jenna's heart.

She was so glad Mel was finally getting her dream man, a little envious all of a sudden that it wasn't her, but still glad for her best friend.

Jenna stood behind Melissa and started to unbutton the back of the dress, trying to hide her moment of weakness from Melissa. She still hadn't figured out a way to tell her about her and Ben and was scared that her face would give away that she was keeping a secret. She knew if Melissa asked this time, she would spill the truth, and now wasn't the time to do it. She had to wait until after Mel came back from her honeymoon.

Jenna lowered the dress to the ground. "Step out."

Melissa stepped over the dress, got off the pedestal, and started to put her regular clothes back on.

"Blair will be green with envy when she sees my dress. While we were at the florist, she kept showing me wedding gowns worth well over fifty K. She was setting up dates to go try them on."

"What, why?"

"She believes Paul is going to pop the question."

"Are you serious?" Jenna had just finished placing the gown back on the body form and looked at Melissa through the mirror. "How do you feel about it?"

Behind her, Melissa was buttoning the last button on her blouse when she looked up at Jenna and met her eyes in the mirror. Melissa frowned, and her cheeks flushed as she plopped down on the settee behind her, pulling Snickerdoodle out of her tote bag.

"It's kind of weird. I know I never really loved Paul, and I'm glad our relationship didn't work out because I would never be marrying Jake otherwise, but we were together six years, and he and Blair have only dated a handful of months. I have this skewed way of thinking and keep wondering what was wrong with me that he didn't want to be married to me."

Jenna turned around and moved beside Melissa faster than lighting.

Melissa looked about to cry. "What is wrong with me? I love Jake. I do, and not once have I questioned our relationship."

Jenna gave her a questioning stare. Melissa gave a wet chuckle as the tears started.

"Okay, I don't count that misunderstanding in high school."

Jenna quirked her eyebrow again.

"Or last Christmas when I nearly let him go again."

They both laughed. But Melissa turned serious again, bringing Snickerdoodle closer to her face, kissing the dog on the head and rubbing her cheek on it afterward. "I'm so embarrassed. Why do I even care about Paul and Blair? They are perfect for each other. I can't believe I even dated him for so long."

"Girl, you're preaching to the choir. I never did understand your relationship with him. It always seemed more out of convenience than anything else. I don't think I could ever do that."

Melissa breathed out heavily. "It was convenient, that is for sure. I'm just being weird. I really do love Jake."

"You don't have to try and convince me. I know you love him. I see it in everything you say or do. You two are meant for each other. But don't beat yourself up over your feelings. They are what they are, and they don't need any rhyme or reason. You may not have loved Paul, but you did spend six years of your life with him."

Melissa nodded.

Then Jenna had an epiphany of what would help Mel get out of her funk. "Okay, I got it."

"What have you got?"

"A question that will stop all this self-doubt."

Melissa moved Snickerdoodle down onto her lap. "I don't have any self-doubt. I am marrying Jake."

Jenna smiled. "Good, but just to make sure you believe yourself, in all the time you dated Paul, did you ever once daydream of marrying him?"

"No, absolutely not."

"See, you answered that so fast that there is no way you are envious of Blair."

"*Eww!* Jenna, I am definitely not envious of Blair. She is a nightmare."

"See?" Jenna tapped Melissa's knee. "Honestly, if you want my opinion, I think if anything Blair is jealous of you. She was probably trying to show you all those gowns to compete because she believes Max is designing the gown. He never designs women's clothing, and everyone in the industry has been trying to get him to for years. Blair is jealous beyond measure because your gown is a once-in-a-lifetime."

"Jenna, I love you. Thank you for saying that. But she is wrong, you know. Max didn't design the gown. You did, and it is one of a kind. You made it, especially for me, and it is beyond stunning. I wish you would let me tell everyone."

"I don't know. Maybe if everyone is raving over it, I might. You never know. You battled your fears of event planning again. Maybe I can overcome mine too."

"You're darn tootin' you can, and I think you are right about Blair. She kept trying to get me to tell her about the dress. Her plan backfired, though, because I ended up shutting down instead. Poor Jake had no idea what was the matter when I got home. I've been acting like such a fool."

Melissa gasped all of a sudden then groaned. "Oh no. Oh no!" Mel started breathing heavily as if she were about to have a panic attack.

"Slow, deep breaths, Mel." Jenna took a few slow ones, helping Melissa.

When Mel was less panicked, she pulled Snickerdoodle back up to her chest. "Jenna, I need to apologize."

Mel looked pitiful. She couldn't imagine why she seemed

almost scared of her, and that was making Jenna worry. "What? Why?"

It took Melissa a few seconds to speak, but her words came out rushed and practically a whisper. "I was so ashamed of my mixed-up feelings about Paul that I couldn't explain them to Jake without sounding horrible. I didn't want him to think I was having second thoughts, so I pinned all my upside-down emotions on you and told him you were depressed again, like back-in-college-depressed."

"What? Mel, why that of all things?"

"I know. It just came out. It seemed like the most logical reason I would seem upset at the time. And when you told me that you were down the night you met Ben the first time, I guess I just exaggerated it, leading him to believe, you know..."

Jenna turned to Melissa, confused. She vaguely remembered giving her that excuse because she was looking for Ben that night and had been late, and he'd been with them all along.

"What? Mel, I'm lost."

Melissa gave her a sympathetic look. "You know, because you were in love and because you didn't want to meet Ben even though I've been trying to get y'all to meet."

Jenna felt herself turn cold and whispered. "What are you talking about?"

Mel looked guilty. Jenna recognized that expression on her face. It was exactly like the time when they were in seventh grade, and they took some candy from Walter's place. Jenna tried to lie about it, but Melissa had already spilled the truth.

"What are you saying? Mel, tell me."

Melissa took a deep breath. "Okay." She took another deep breath and closed her eyes, squeezing them tight. "I know about New York."

Jenna felt like she was about to faint. That wasn't what she expected Melissa to say.

She could barely get her voice out now. "What?"

Melissa opened her eyes, and they were cloudy with tears. "Don't get mad. I know you were heartbroken and came home to mend. That's why when Jake was in the hospital, we came up with the plan to get you and Ben together. You were both hurt so badly that we felt like maybe, just maybe, we could have you accidentally meet as if it were serendipity."

Jenna swallowed hard, and tears formed in her eyes at the betrayal from her best friend keeping that knowledge. All this time, she had been beating herself up about what a horrible friend she was by not telling Melissa about Ben. Her feelings felt so mixed up. She was upset at herself for not telling and upset for looking like a fool, because all this time Melissa knew, and she was still her friend.

Then she felt betrayed again when she thought how Melissa and Jake couldn't have planned their little game if they didn't know from the source. Ben lied. He did tell Jake. How could she ever trust him again? He wasn't the man she believed him to be. He was faking this whole time, probably as payback for her playing her stupid games.

Jenna got up. "I'm sorry, Mel. I can't do this now," she said and walked out of her office then out to the front of her store.

Max called out to her as she opened the door to leave. "Darling, where are you going?"

Jenna stopped at the door and Melissa had made her way up front. Her face conveyed her remorse as she held Snickerdoodle in one arm and placed her hand on Max's forearm and shook her head. "Let her go. Can you lock up the shop for her?"

The second Jenna heard Max say "Sure," she ran to her car and drove home. It felt like the world she just built up had come crumbling down, and with it, every ounce of her happiness.

CHAPTER TWENTY

*B*en and Jake were grilling steaks on the patio when Melissa came out the back door in tears. She placed her dog on the ground and it ran off to play in the yard.

Jake handed Ben the tongs and opened his arms for Melissa to curl into them. "Lissy, what's wrong?"

"I was an idiot. I told Jenna that I knew why she came home from New York depressed and that you and I decided to try and get her and Ben to meet up by chance before the wedding."

Ben dropped the metal tongs. They clattered loudly on the grill. Jake and Melissa turned to him as he fumbled to pick them up.

"Oh, Ben," Melissa gushed. "I'm so sorry. Jake and I knew that you and Jenna were perfect for one another the moment we started talking about you both having a similar past. I never meant to hurt you or Jenna by my interference. I just hope that me opening my big mouth hasn't made everything worse and you won't end up even more awkward around each other."

Ben was trying to get what Melissa was saying organized in his brain. Did she know about him and Jenna or just believe

Jenna had a broken heart? How could he ask without giving himself away and breaking Jenna's trust by accident?

"What exactly did you tell her?" Jake took the words out of Ben's mouth.

Ben turned the steaks then went to the outdoor table where Jake and Melissa had migrated and sat down.

"I told her that you and I were trying to make a moment of serendipity for her, a setup where it was like she and Ben met by chance."

Jake sighed. "Lissy, even though I agreed. I thought we said we wouldn't interfere."

Melissa sniffled. "We did, but I ended up trying to mess with fate."

Ben swore and rubbed his hand in his hair. Both Melissa and Jake turned to Ben. "Sorry." He was afraid to say more, racking his brain to remember if he ever told Jake about the game. It didn't make sense, and he blurted out, "I don't understand, how could me meeting Jenna at your wedding be serendipitous?"

Melissa deflated. Her face turned beet red. "Well, it actually started a few months back. Ever since Jenna told me she wanted to meet someone where it was easy, that she wanted love just to happen, I figured playing a little game of chance might give it a push start. But it didn't work. We never ran into Ben." She glanced at Ben apologetically and wiped her eyes with the edge of her sleeve. "Gosh, I'm so embarrassed."

Ben's mind was spinning.

"Lissy," Jake admonished.

"I know, but Jenna had no idea. I mean, it's not like she didn't visit me all the time when I lived there, and with what I do in event planning it wasn't far-reaching that I would want to use my contacts and take Jenna on trips to the city."

Both Ben and Jake stared at Melissa as she rambled.

"Y'all, don't look at me like I have two heads. Seriously, it's not uncommon for people to go into the city and shop for their wedding. I just thought I'd, you know, hit two birds with one stone and purposely go places near your old job," she said directly to Jake and then lifted her shoulders, her cheeks once again pink, directing her eyes to Ben.

"And we'd have lunch at restaurants I knew you specifically went to, hoping to run into you by chance."

So it *was* Jenna Ben had seen all those times. He couldn't believe this. He laughed out loud. Melissa gave Ben a wavering smile. More than anything, Melissa admitting this gave Ben a sense of validation. The sensation was quite heady, and he couldn't wait to call his therapist and tell her he wasn't crazy after all. Well, Dr. Archer never called him crazy. Now he knew that more than likely, he really had been seeing Jenna. Ben sat quietly, listening to the buzz of Melissa as she apologized again, and he felt himself nodding, accepting her apology, but he couldn't make words come out. His mind was too consumed with retracing the timeline to when he started having hallucinations of Jenna. He heard Jake say something, reassuring Melissa that Jenna would forgive her and everything would be alright, and encouraged her to text Jenna her apology.

Ben decided that he needed to check on Jenna. He had to make sure that she understood he didn't tell Melissa about their past. He stood up, went to check the steak, then turned the grill off. He placed the steaks on the serving dish, and as he laid it on the table, "Guys, why don't you both have dinner together? I have some last-minute things I need to do for work."

Jake stood up. "Ben, you don't have to leave. Plus, you're supposed to be on holiday, not working."

"This work is for my personal future as well as that of the company. It's alright."

Jake nodded. "Fine, but don't stay at Walter's until closing again. You really are supposed to take a break every now and then."

"Yes, Umma."

Jake threw a wadded-up napkin at his head, but Ben caught it and tossed it back at Jake so fast Jake didn't see it coming and it hit him right between the eyes. "Dude, you nearly blinded me."

The three of them laughed, finally breaking the heavy tension.

It didn't take long for Ben to arrive at Jenna's house. The sun was about to set, and the temperature had dropped some, but Jenna was sitting on her front step, leaning her head on the railing post. She had on some cut-off shorts and no shoes with a light shawl wrapped around her shoulders. The minute she saw his car stop and him get out, she ran inside the house. He heard the lock click as he ran after her.

He knocked on the door and waited. "Jenna, I know you're in there. Melissa told Jake and me what happened. Please let me in."

Ben waited for a good five minutes with no answer. He walked around to the back door to see if she had gone into the kitchen. "Jenna, please let me in. I promise Melissa still doesn't know about us if that's what you're worried about."

Still no response. Ben didn't know what to do. What if he was wrong? What if Melissa did know it was him? He decided to find Walter and Max to get their opinion.

It didn't take him long to rush into Main Street Java and find Max and Walter sitting at a table talking.

"Hey Ben, I thought you and Jake were staying in tonight."

Ben pulled out a seat from the table beside them and brought the chair to their table. "We were, but something happened, and I need to ask you both something."

Max nodded, and Walter responded, "Sure, son."

"Did either of you mention anything about Jenna and me to

Melissa or Jake? About us?" He turned to look around the cafe and whispered, "Before, back in New York."

Both men just stared at Ben as he started drumming his fingers on the table.

Max finally broke the silence. "Not to my recollection. Jenna forbade me to mention anything even though I told that girl playing games with people never leads to anything good. What exactly happened?"

Ben then turned to Walter who said, "I may tend to talk a lot, but I can guarantee I've been too caught up in my own drama to talk about Jenna's."

Max patted Walter's hand across the table then asked Ben, "You feel like telling us what happened?"

Ben relayed everything he knew and when he finished, Max turned to him. "I can tell you right now, Jenna thinks you talked," he said thoughtfully.

Ben slumped in his seat. "When she ran into the house and didn't answer the door, that's what my gut told me too. How in the world am I supposed to get her to listen to me now?"

"Darling," Max said to Ben, "Jenna is going to have to open up and talk to Melissa. She has to grow up and face all her insecurities. I'll work on her, and you…" He patted Ben on the cheek. "Be patient with her. I have a feeling that she will see the light in a few days."

Walter agreed, "I've known Jenna for a long time, and that girl is as giddy as they get, but I have never seen her as happy as when she is with you, son. Plus, with you moving here soon, if she continues to be this stubborn, seeing you around town will eventually break her down."

Ben tried to smile. "I hope I didn't make a mistake when I bought the space from you. All I kept thinking about was building my dream here and being with Jenna again. It'll be hard to stay if she wants nothing to do with me."

"I won't keep you to the purchase agreement if things do fall through with Jenna. Let's put it on hold for a couple of months for you to be certain. It's not like the place has had anyone interested in it in the last thirty years. Except for Melissa, of course."

Ben groaned. "You'll probably get at least a few others begging for it once they see what she has done with the place. The transformation with the decor she's rented is quite impressive for a hollowed-out shell of a building."

Max agreed, "That girl has a gift. I certainly could have used her back in the day when I had to host events."

Ben turned to Max. "So, you really are giving up everything to move back here?"

Walter kicked Ben's foot under the table, and Ben turned to a scowling Walter. "Don't you be placing any ideas in his head to go back other than to pack. I waited too long for him to come back home."

Max clasped Walter's hand in his. "I won't change my mind." Then turned to Ben. "I'm seventy years old. I'm ready to retire and live the quiet life and help Walter with the cafe."

"I may not be able to retire. I finally got my dad on my side about what I'd like to do here, but I sure wish I didn't have this horrible sense of dread growing in the pit of my stomach telling me that my dream was just that, a dream."

The three men sat in silence for a good while until Ben stood up and placed his chair back at the other table. "Thanks for your time. I think I'll head back to Jake's."

Max and Walter stood up and walked Ben out. Max cuffed him on the shoulder affectionately. "I'll pry what I can out of her and keep you posted."

Ben smiled warmly at Max, genuinely liking the man more and more as he got to know him. "Thanks." And, impulsively, he felt the need to hug the older man, so he did.

"You're a good man, Ben. We'll make Jenna see reason."

CHAPTER TWENTY-ONE

*T*he morning of the wedding arrived, and Ben met his parents for breakfast at the B and B. They arrived late the evening before, but Ben didn't have time to see them because of the wedding rehearsal and dinner. That was the most awkward experience of his life, and he felt horrible for Melissa and Jake.

Jenna was sweet to Melissa, although you could tell it was strained, and she completely ignored him except when she had to walk with him down the aisle when executing the practice march. She was stiff as a board and stared straight ahead, ignoring every word he said.

He even told her that Melissa didn't know it was him and that all she had done was speculate based on basic clues. Jenna didn't budge in her stubbornness. Max had told him to be patient, but when Jenna acted like a petulant child, Ben felt so old compared to her.

"Benjamin," his mom called when she saw him arrive.

She was already standing with her arms open, waiting for a hug. Smiling, he stooped down, hugging his mom and joking. "Are you shrinking again?"

"Oh, you," she swatted him on his arm. "Why do you always have to pick on your Umma?"

His dad stood up and hugged him and told his wife, "Because he wouldn't be my son if he didn't."

His mom smiled. "You two will be the death of me. But it sure is good to see you both smiling again with each other rather than on opposite sides about work."

Ben plucked the biscuit off his mom's plate and took a bite, winking at her. "I have to agree it's nice to be on the same page finally."

"That it is," his dad agreed. "Speaking of, last night we popped on over to Main Street Java and asked Walter if we could have a look at the space."

Even though his dad wanted to look at the location from a business perspective, his mom placed her hand over her chest. "The reception will be beautiful. I can't wait to see the bride. I heard Maximilian Thorne designed her gown and is in town."

"Where in the world did you hear that?" Ben turned to his mom. He knew very well Jenna had designed the dress. Was she playing games with that too? She never told him that she wanted Max to take credit.

His mom fanned her face with her hand. "I met a celebrity!"

"You met Max?"

"No, but I wouldn't mind meeting that hunk."

Both Ben and his dad both groaned.

Ben said, "Umma!"

At the same time, his dad said, "I don't need to hear about your man-crush."

Ben laughed at his dad.

"Stop it, you two. I can have a crush if I want to. I'm old enough and happy in my marriage, so no need to worry. Anyway, I met a YouTuber. Blair Kinkade, have you seen her?"

"No, I haven't, but I've heard all about her."

His mom gushed on and on about Blair and how wonderful

she was, which was in complete opposition to what he had heard from Jenna, Melissa, and Jake. But who was he to destroy his mom's happiness?

When she noticed Ben wasn't paying attention or eating his breakfast, she asked, "Benny, are you still worried about the girl?" She looked around the table, making sure no one heard. Ben had told his parents that he found Jenna again and that she hadn't told her friend about them, so he was keeping it quiet, and also that she was currently upset with him because of a misunderstanding.

"Yeah, I'm hoping today goes well for Jake. I don't want to ruin any part of his wedding because of issues with Jenna and me."

"I don't know what's wrong with that girl. Look at you, a fine, sharply dressed, hardworking man who, like his father, is a teddy bear to be around."

Ben's dad gave her a sharp look. "Hey now. I am not soft."

"No, you are hard as a rock, sometimes a bit too serious, but your heart is softer than the sweetest little bear on earth."

Ben's dad rolled his eyes, but a soft smile tilted the corner of his lips. He was a softy for anything about Ben's mom.

"Anyway, Benny, you just be you and have fun at the wedding. You don't need that girl to keep you happy. Ah, look…"

His mom shot up and started waving at someone entering the dining area. She was a tall, slender woman who was quite stunning, and Ben's first instinct was to stand up out of respect. Then his mom called out her name. "Blair! Come and join us."

So, this was Blair. Up close, even though she was gorgeous, the moment she started talking and droning on and on about herself, he knew that once more, no one, not even someone as stunning as she was, could take his mind off of Jenna.

By the time breakfast was over, Ben had tuned out most of the conversation and discovered too late that he had said yes to accompanying Blair from the church to the reception — scowling at his mom for even suggesting the idea. She was fangirling a little too much for his comfort, and because of his poor attention span, he fell right into her trap. He tried to focus on the conversation and rolled his eyes when Blair patted a fake tear of gratitude at his mother's offer for him to be her last-minute date since her coworker had to go back to the office for an impromptu meeting with a new sponsor. For some reason, he could have sworn that Melissa told him that her coworker was Blair's boyfriend and Melissa's ex. Too much drama for him to handle. He turned to his dad, who was looking at his phone hidden under the table, scanning the stock market.

Ben couldn't help but elbow his dad, trying to knock the phone out of his hand.

The phone almost flew out, but his dad still had terrific reflexes and caught it. He turned to Ben, giving him a pensive look.

Ben leaned toward his dad's ear and in a low voice said, "I meant to tell you that I heard from the realtor this morning. Not only do we have an offer for the office, but I found a buyer for my house."

When he sat back, he watched his dad's eyes widen. "So, you're really doing this?"

"Yes." Tension filled his gut when his dad frowned.

His dad breathed out a sigh and spoke softly so the ladies wouldn't hear. "I knew this day would come, that one day I would retire, and you'd take over. It's definitely not what I envisioned, but times are changing, as everyone keeps reminding me."

He put his hand on Ben's shoulder. "I'm proud of you, son, for going after your dreams. I just hope this girl you're holding out for is worth the investment of our company."

Ben choked up. His dad rarely ever told him he was proud of him and his choices. But it was the last part that really got to him. His dad was letting him have the money from the company to do with as he wished, invest it in his bookstore and publishing house here in Cypressville.

Ben swallowed the lump in his throat and whispered, "Thanks, Dad. That means more to me than you will ever know."

His dad clapped his hand on Ben's knee and cleared his throat. "Joon, I believe it's time we head out for that country drive before we need to get back for the wedding, and Ben needs to head to Jake's to get ready." His dad stood and turned to Blair. "Nice to meet you." Then he walked over to Joon to help her out of her seat.

Ben stood and gave his mom a hug farewell. He nodded to Blair. "Well, I guess I'll see you after the wedding, but my mother really shouldn't have volunteered me, being that I am in the wedding party. I have to admit I was lost in thought when I agreed." Plus, he worried how it would look to Jenna. He said a silent prayer she wouldn't misunderstand.

Blair laughed. It seemed fake. She placed her hand on his chest, acting all coy. "Oh Benjamin, your mother is a dear. I know you and I will hit it off beautifully." She leaned in to kiss him on the cheek, just as Jenna came into the dining area.

Jenna's face turned a nasty shade of puce. Even from this distance, he could see tears fill her eyes. He shook Blair off and chased after Jenna, hollering her name for him to stop.

The disappearing act she was so good at in the past happened again. He had no clue where she went or why she was even at the B and B, but he knew that what she just witnessed probably screwed up any chance of them getting back together. Everything looked so bad and he didn't know if telling the truth would even help.

CHAPTER TWENTY-TWO

*J*enna couldn't breathe. She'd snuck into the alleyway between the B and B and Mr. Simon's Antique Shop. Letting her tears fall freely, she squatted on the ground behind a bush, waiting for Ben to either pass by or give up looking for her. What had she been thinking, going to search him out on the morning of Melissa's wedding?

Last night Melissa had her on the phone, rambling on and on about what needed to be done in the morning. First, they would need to get to the church by one o'clock to get ready there. Andrea and Jenna would be helping her get ready. Thank goodness Andrea had prohibited Blair from coming.

In the background, Jenna had heard Ben's voice and tried to zero in on what he was saying to Jake. Was he missing her as much as she missed him? Her hopes were dashed away when he only asked Jake if it was okay to meet his parents for breakfast at the B and B before he and Jake started to get ready.

After she hung up with Melissa, she had a serious talk with herself. Melissa tried to apologize, and Jenna stopped her in her tracks. Her words to Melissa still rang in her ears: "You don't need forgiving. I do, for not trusting you with the truth a long time ago. I thought I could get over it better if I pretended it never happened. I mean, although it was easy love, it was short-spanned. Really, who falls in love that fast?"

Melissa had tried to talk, but Jenna shut her down by changing the topic to the wedding.

It had worked, and Melissa never brought it up again. Max and Walter, on the other hand, kept pestering her to hear Ben out. After hearing his voice over the phone, she decided to take their advice and go surprise Ben to try and get him alone for just a few minutes to explain.

From the way Max and Walter talked, she had completely misunderstood the entire situation. It upset her that they didn't just automatically take her side as she expected. Max even called her mom and dad and told them the whole story. Later that same night, she got a call telling her that she was twenty-seven years old and needed to stop playing games and grow up. She needed to hear what the young man had to say and make an educated decision based on fact, not the imaginings and created scenarios of her mind.

Deep down, she knew everyone was right. So, this morning, she decided she would suck it up, put her big girl pants on and quit playing games. After hearing Ben's side of the story, if it seemed plausible, she would give him her number and ask him on a date. Hopefully by her taking the initiative, he would understand she was ready to commit.

But the moment she walked in and saw Blair on his arm kissing him, dread set in. Her worst nightmare had happened. Falling in love again only to be proven she can't ever trust her judgment with men. She would stay single the rest of her life because this was all too hard. This was the reason she played games. It kept her safe.

So, she sat, only hours before her best friend's wedding, crying in a bush.

Melissa would for sure know something was wrong when she saw her. Her puffy eyes would be the giveaway.

Her phone rang. She sniffed and wiped her eyes, cleared her throat, put on her best fake cheerful voice, and answered. "Hey girl, happy wedding day!"

Melissa was rushing about, muttering on and on about how she didn't have any bobby pins. "Mel, breathe. You don't need any. Jilly is bringing them when she comes to do your hair and makeup at three." She listened to Melissa apologize then freak out over some other minor detail that Jenna had to reassure her had been taken care of. That went on for a few minutes when Jenna finally had enough. "Mel, now listen to me and listen to me carefully. Stop worrying about everything. It's all done, and what isn't done, you won't remember the minute you are walking down the aisle and see Jake at the altar waiting for you. That man is what today is about. It's about your forever, not the tiny details of this or that being done."

Melissa was crying over the line now. Jenna started crying again, her heart aching at the happiness she felt for her best friend and the fear of putting on a smile for Ben when she knew that her happy ending was possibly interested in Blair, or so it seemed. Before her tears turned to anger, she rushed Mel off the phone.

"I love you, girl. See you in a couple of hours, and remember, don't shampoo your hair when you shower."

Hanging up, she started to think horrible thoughts about the two-timing Blair. First, she wants Paul, and now that she has him, she is discarding him for Jenna's man. Second, Ben was really attractive, way better looking than Paul. Even though Paul was handsome in his own way, Ben was more handsome. Third, his personality was a little dorky but incredibly endearing. She loved how he wore his heart on his sleeve when he was with her. So why was she struggling to see it now?

Was she that jaded? All her games were just great big walls

she'd built up around her heart. Playing them for so long had changed her so much that she didn't see what was right in front of her.

She should have confided in Mel a long time ago. If she had, she wouldn't have started the game pretending she and Ben didn't know one another. But just because they were having fun together didn't make them a couple. She hated how her mind kept changing.

Jenna blew out a breath and whispered to the cat that walked by. "Today is Melissa's day. I will forget about Ben, and after today I won't have to see him again because he is going back to his life in publishing." In New Orleans, three and a half hours away, a city which she has no intention of ever moving to. She got over him once she could get over him again.

Jenna got up and sneaked her way back to her car, looking every which way, praying Ben had given up looking for her.

CHAPTER TWENTY-THREE

*M*ax and Jenna arrived at the church carrying Melissa and Jenna's gowns and all the accessories. "Darling, do you want me to stay and help style you both?"

Jenna gave Max her first genuine smile of the day. "No, you go home to style yourself. You probably need more time than Mel and I put together."

He returned her grin with his own and a wink. "True, darling." He bent down and kissed her on the cheek. "I'll be seeing you in a few hours then."

Thankfully he didn't mention Ben.

Melissa and her stepmother, Andrea, weren't there yet, so she took both gowns out of the garment bags, pulled out her clothes steamer, and removed any last-minute wrinkles. When Jilly, the cosmetologist arrived, Jenna looked at her watch then at Jilly. "Did you see Melissa anywhere?"

"No, I was surprised to see only you here getting things ready."

Jenna picked up her phone and dialed.

Melissa answered, sounding panicked. "We got a flat! Dad didn't have a spare. We called triple-A."

Jenna heard a little bark over the phone. "I thought you decided not to bring Snickerdoodle because you didn't want her to get hurt in the crowd."

"I did, but I was so stressed out this morning, crying and freaking out over the tiniest of things, that Dad brought her kennel to the reception area already, set it up, and I called Susan. She is going to hold her during the wedding. Oh, thank goodness!"

Melissa sounded relieved. Jenna could hear a lot of talking in the background and her curiosity got the best of her. "What? What's happening? Don't leave me hanging."

"Susan just pulled up. She and Megan are going to bring Andrea and me to the church. Jake told her where we were, and she U-turned to come get us. Gosh, I love that man. He is always taking care of me."

Jenna heard Melissa's dad say, "Hey now," and Andrea soothe him.

Jenna could hear a smile in Melissa's voice. "Dad and Snickky will wait for triple-A and meet us later."

Fifteen minutes after they hung up, a flustered Melissa, a bouncing excited Megan, and a calm and cool Susan rushed into the room. Susan was carrying her and Megan's dresses.

When Susan spotted Melissa's gown, Jenna could see the admiration in her eyes. She turned to Jenna, "This is the most stunning gown I have ever seen. Tell your uncle it is utterly gorgeous."

Jenna felt her cheeks flush, and Mel came up next to Jenna and whispered, "You need to tell everyone it was you who designed the dress."

Neither Jenna nor Melissa realized Megan was hiding under the skirt of the gown until she shouted, "Jenna, you made this?"

Susan fussed when she saw where her daughter was playing. "Megan, get out from under that gown immediately! If you soil it, so help me..."

Megan giggled and scurried out from under the dress before her mom reached her. Then she took off, practically bouncing all around the room as if she had eaten an entire bowl of sugar saturated in caffeine.

Susan shook her head in exasperation. "That girl is too excited for her own good." She ignored her child's display and turned to Jenna. "You designed this? Did you sew it also?"

Melissa nodded for Jenna. The room erupted into a cacophony of sound as all three women started talking. Melissa apologized over and over. Susan and Jilly begged for more details. Andrea was one step ahead of everyone, trying to calm Melissa, seeing that she was near to hyperventilating, while all Jenna could seem to do was stand there frozen as if she were stuck in some alternate reality.

This day was supposed to be special. She was supposed to be able to celebrate her best friend's wedding, but somehow it got all screwed up, and all of her worst fears spilled out into the universe, and now she had to face them. But first, she had to snap out of it and go to Mel. She needed to make sure she was alright. Jenna forced herself to answer the girls.

"Yes, I designed it. I'm not ready to go public, so please don't mention it." She pushed between the two women as they protested, saying she shouldn't hide such talent, but her thoughts were focused on turning this off of her and back to her best friend. She would not continue to ruin Melissa's wedding day.

"Mel, it's okay. I promise." Jenna squatted down beside Melissa, who was leaning back in a chair with her head resting on the back of it.

Andrea came back with a cold bottle of water and handed it to Melissa. "Here you go."

Melissa opened one eye and sat up straighter, took the water, and took a sip.

Andrea said, "Listen to Jenna, honey. She wouldn't lie to you. If she said it's okay, then it's okay. Today is your wedding day."

She looked at her watch and turned to Jilly. "We need to start getting our hair done if we want to keep on schedule."

Jenna felt like such a heel. She was a liar and needed to be straight with Melissa. Now didn't seem to be the time to get into all the details, but at least she could apologize for evading the truth all these years.

She grabbed Melissa's hand. "I'm sorry I never told you about Ben and for making you keep the dress a secret I don't know why I am the way I am, but it's okay that you and everyone knows. Today is your day, and I want you to be happy. Can we just forget all of this and get you ready to be Mrs. Blessing?"

Melissa squeezed her hand and hugged her. "Absolutely! She leaned back and held her pinky out to Jenna. Her eyes had brightened and a wicked grin appeared, taking the place of her anxiety. "And promise you'll tell me your juicy secret about Ben."

Her voice sounded as if she were surprised, confusing Jenna. But she didn't want to talk about it with everyone around. "Sure thing," she said and returned the smile with a wavering one of her own.

"Good, I was so hoping you two would hit it off and erase the pain of your past. And promise me you will never keep secrets from me again. It was tough pretending I didn't know you dated some random guy back then who broke your heart. Good thing I didn't know his name, or I might have sent him an email telling him off."

Jilly came to Melissa, interrupting them. "Ready."

Melissa jumped up out of her seat, smiling as if nothing had happened. The joy of her wedding returned. Jenna plopped into the chair Melissa just left, thoroughly confused. It seemed that Mel didn't know the guy in college was Ben. He hadn't told her.

Gosh, was she ever a fool! She should have let him explain the other day. Then the image of Blair kissing his cheek popped into her head and her jealousy flared up again. Susan sat beside her at the perfect time. Jenna decided that no matter what happened today, she would redirect her thoughts at all costs to keep the wedding happy.

"Jenna, I'm sorry about earlier. I just, the dress is stunning and —" Megan came up to her mom, leaned on her side, and interrupted, adding in her two cents. "It's true, Jenna. It is bee-you-ti-full."

Jenna couldn't help but feel pride from their praise. She knew the dress came out well. Max wouldn't stop raving about her talents and even told her that he would talk to some of his people if she'd like to have a trunk show one day. The thought only recently started to not scare her, strangely, since she and Ben had been spending time together. His encouragement and look of amazement on his face when he watched her as she sketched out new designs or worked on Melissa's gown was the look of amazement. He was one of the only other people she told about her skills.

The initial fear of everyone finding out a few moments ago had been more of a programmed reaction. Now, after she saw Blair trying to steal Ben away this morning, she was more than ready to make that woman eat humble pie.

CHAPTER TWENTY-FOUR

*J*ake stood at the back of the church, taking deep breaths and pacing.

Ben just got word from Frank that Melissa was on her way out for the couple's first look and photo. "Hey, man."

Jake stopped his pacing, and his face lit up with joy. "Is this it? Is she about to come out?"

"Yes."

Jake breathed out and rubbed his hand down his chest, resting on his abdomen for a second. "It's not like I haven't been here before, but goodness, I'm a bundle of nerves."

Concerned over Jake's words, Ben found himself questioning if he needed to help Jake do a runner. "Good nerves I hope."

"Absolutely good nerves. I'm about to marry the woman I've dreamed about since I was sixteen."

Ben grinned widely. "Good, but just so that you know, I would have helped you run if it were the other kind of nerves."

Jake gave him a stunned, sharp look, then his features relaxed. "Thanks, man. That tells me one thing."

"What would that be? That I'm obnoxious for not having faith in you?"

"No, man, that you really are my friend if you'd let me do a runner and clean up the mess."

Andrea walked around the corner and, in a firm, clipped voice, said, "I sure hope I heard that in the wrong context, boys."

They both chucked. Jake turned around. Jenna had fashioned another beautiful gown. Andrea had on a satin floor-length off-shoulder gown, and it hugged all the right curves. "Andrea, you look stunning, as pretty as a bride."

"Oh, hush, you. Frank is bringing Melissa." Andrea then turned to the young man who came with the photographer, who was preoccupied with his phone. She snapped her fingers and in a loud, firm voice said, "If you are helping your mother with the pictures, get off that phone and get your camera ready. It's time to get the groom in place. His bride is coming."

"Yes, ma'am. I mean, yes, mayor ma'am." The young man fumbled with his lens, looking up apologetically. "Sorry, this is the first wedding my mom let me help on. I'm a bit nervous."

Jake, Ben, and Andrea all turned to the young man, who seemed to get more and more flustered with all their attention on him. With the camera hanging from his neck the young man started rambling, "No, no, no, don't worry." He waved his hands frantically, sputtering out excuses for not paying attention. "I'm not going to screw up the pictures. I'm sorry I was on my phone. Please don't tell my mom. I promised her I was ready for this chance, and Miss Melissa was really nice letting me come help."

The poor kid's face was splotching. The three adults all turned to one another and chuckled. Jake thankfully put the kid out of misery. "No worries," he said as he walked over to the young man. Jake looped his arm over the kid's shoulders, and relief seemed to pour out of the boy as he exhaled. Andrea turned to the young photographer and said, "Yes, yes, there is nothing to worry about."

"Come on, show me where your mom wants me." Jake winked

at Ben and Andrea as he walked to the small atrium in the church entrance.

Ben turned to Andrea. "I was just joking. He's more than ready to marry Melissa."

Andrea gave a chuckle. "You don't have to explain. I know that boy is ready to marry Melissa. Those two were made for each other. God rest her soul, but little Molly never did seem the right fit for him." Then she turned and walked off.

Ben stood there almost dumbfounded at her words. He didn't quite know what to make of them.

He figured if he planned on settling there, he'd have to get used to the folks in this part of the woods being a bit free in giving out more information than you asked for compared to back home.

The small church was just outside of town, and Ben surveyed the countryside. Home. How odd that soon his house wouldn't be in the hustle and bustle of a large metropolis but instead in a small town where the nearest city was thirty to forty minutes away. There was a small part of him that worried if he was making the right decision.

His phone buzzed in his pocket. He started to ignore it as he walked toward the church but decided to answer at the last minute. His assistant knew he was at the wedding and would only call if it was important.

"Hello"

"Ben. I'm sorry to call you, but it's your mom and dad."

Ben's heart stopped in his chest. "What?" he choked out.

"I got a call from the hospital. Your parents were in an accident about an hour ago and were brought to the hospital in Alexandria."

Ben felt like his whole world was crumbling. He sat on the step and couldn't breathe as he waited for her to finish.

"Before you worry, they are both alright, hardly even a scratch, but because your dad's heart rate was erratic and your mom was hysterical with worry and had a panic attack, they brought them both in for evaluation. Your dad left his phone in the console of the car that's been towed, and your mom left hers at the B and B."

"So, to be clear, they are, okay?"

"Oh gosh, Ben, yes, yes, I'm so bad at this. I told your dad to let me give him your number for him to call, but the nurse came in and he got agitated and told me to tell you they were going to miss the wedding. They asked if when it was over, you could go and get them. He said they'd probably still be there because of all the tests they were running."

Ben breathed a sigh of relief. "Thanks for letting me know. I'll get there as soon as I can."

"Again, sorry, Ben."

"Thanks for calling. I'm glad you did."

"Oh, while I have you on the line, and I know this is a huge change of topic, but I was planning to call you later this evening when I knew the wedding was over."

He stood up to start heading into the church.

"The closing for the sale of the building is going to be Monday at eight-thirty, and the closing agent said that they should be able to close on both your house and the office the same day. I blocked out your morning. Do you want me to hire you some movers to clear out your house for you?"

"Dang, that was way faster than I was expecting."

"The realtor and the closing attorney reassured me that both buyers would give you until the end of the month to clear out all of your belongings from the office and your house."

"Thanks, and yes, line up the movers for my house, and also could you find one for the office too while you're at it? Tomorrow, I'll give you the details of where I will be storing everything. I wasn't expecting the closing for another few weeks, so I will need to head into the office when the wedding is over. I know tomorrow is Sunday, but can I talk you into meeting me there around ten to finalize some things to get it ready for the movers?"

"Sure, Tony shouldn't mind. I'll just send him to the golf range, and he'll be happy as a lark."

"If my dad calls again, let him and my mom know I'll be there as soon as I can break away."

CHAPTER TWENTY-FIVE

*B*en entered the church to the breathtaking vision of Jenna. She wore a pale, rose-colored silk halter gown and was standing off to one side, wiping a tear from her eye. A huge smile graced her lips and she held her hand to her heart as Melissa and Jake had their first looks. Ben was glad he didn't miss it. Jake slowly turned, and Ben saw his Adam's apple bob a few times as he held back his emotions.

Jake reached for Melissa's hand then spun her around. "Simply stunning," were the only words he said as a tear leaked out of his eyes.

Ben was choked up. Melissa was beautiful in the gown Jenna designed. Jenna had a flair for mixing modern and vintage looks. The gown Melissa had on made her look like a movie star, and the pearls that Jenna and Max painstakingly sewed on lined the bodice at the waist, all the way down the sheer upper back of her dress, and down the train. He could feel their love fill the room. Andrea leaned back into her husband and Melissa's dad, Frank, who wrapped his arm around her waist, bringing her closer to him, smiling, not hiding his tears for his one and only daughter.

Slowly, Jake leaned into Melissa, kissed her on her cheek, grabbed her hand, and led her to a small table, set up with a photo of Melissa's mom and a picture of Jake's late wife, Molly. There were two candles in front of the images. The pastor said a prayer, and Jake and Melissa each lit a candle.

The pastor gave each a hug, stepped away, and spoke loudly for the wedding party to hear.

"Melissa, best go touch up your makeup. The guests will be arriving shortly. Jake, you and Ben can come with me to the altar."

Jenna turned to the back of the church where Ben stood. This was the first time he'd seen her in days. She wouldn't stop watching him. Then she mouthed the most beautiful words that eased some of the anxieties of the last few moments: "I'm sorry."

Ben's heart lifted and he smiled at her, nodding.

While Jake and Melissa exchanged vows, Ben couldn't help but get distracted by Jenna. He couldn't wait to talk to her. To one day see her standing at the altar exchanging vows with him. But first, he wanted to make sure she knew that he wasn't going to leave her again, and second he wanted her to meet his parents. Maybe he could get her to come with him to pick up them up. Not that the hospital would be the best place, but he didn't want her out of his sight again. He knew he loved her, and he was ready for his forever. A few more days wouldn't hurt. Once he signed the papers and packed, he'd be in Cypressville permanently, and then he wouldn't leave her side again.

Ben was brought back into the moment when the pastor proclaimed jovially, "You may now kiss the bride!"

That was one thing he envied about Jake. He had found his forever and held on to her. The moment Ben found out Jenna lived here, he made up his mind that he was ready to do the same thing. It never did take him long to learn from his past mistakes. This time he'd profess his feelings and plans to Jenna the moment they had a chance to and talk without the entire church watching.

That chance never seemed to arrive. After the wedding, Blair hovered at the exit like a vulture, reminding him that he was to drive her to the reception. Jenna practically gave him the death glare when she saw him lead Blair to his car. He was sick to his stomach with the thought that Jenna was regretting her apology and would soon ignore him again. The young photographer passed by and Ben grabbed his arm, stopping him in his tracks. "Are you headed to the reception?" Ben asked.

"Yes sir, I am following behind my mom."

"Great! Blair meet..." Ben turned to the boy.

"Everett," the boy responded.

"Everett, would you be ever so kind and give Blair a ride to the reception? I have something I need to attend to and unfortunately, I am unable to."

Blair turned toward where Ben was looking. Jenna was getting in the car with Max and Walter. Blair must have understood, as with the grace of a celebrity she hooked her arm into the young man's. "Thank you so much for the ride. How about we do a little livestream from the car and you can show me a few sneak peaks at the photos on that camera of yours."

Once at the reception, they were swept away to pose for photo after photo. Ben's smile became plastered on as worry built up the longer he wasn't able to talk to Jenna before leaving to get his parents. The dinner started and once more they were on either side of the bride and groom. After Ben made his toast, he hoped to finally get his chance when the dancing began, but before his speech ended his phone buzzed in his pocket.

Ben turned to the side to answer the call. His parents had been released from the hospital and needed to be picked up. His time was up.

The couple that owned the ice rink were at the table talking to Jake and Melissa. "Pardon the intrusion. Jake, got a minute?"

A smiling Jake turned to Ben. Ben explained everything that happened minutes before the wedding that he kept from Jake so as not to ruin his moment.

"Man, had I known..." Jake cuffed Ben affectionately on the shoulder, knowing Ben worried often over his dad's health.

"They are fine, thank goodness. I wanted to talk to Jenna alone. I was hoping to have her come with me, but..." Both men looked around the open space where she was no longer sitting, and looked around the reception area. She was nowhere in sight.

"There's Max and Walter. Why don't you check with them before you leave? If I see her, I'll tell her where you went if you'd like."

"Nah, I'll tell her when I see her."

"Good man, looking on the bright side. Good luck, and thank you for being my best man."

They stood up and Jake held his hand out to Ben, and Ben pulled Jake into a hug.

"I wouldn't have missed this for the world. Enjoy your honeymoon. I'll be a Cypressville citizen when you return."

Jake stopped his retreat. "Wait, so soon? What changed? I thought it would be a few more months yet."

"Same, but when Cynthia called to tell me about my parents' accident, she told me the reason she was in the office on Saturday. The realtor and the attorney needed some papers I had signed and mailed to the office before the closing at 8:30 Monday. She was picking them up and thankfully answered the phone when my dad called."

Jake whistled. "But you still have your house to contend with. Won't that take a while too?"

"Nope, I failed to mention the closing is for both business and personal."

Jake smiled and clapped Ben on the shoulder again. "Welcome to Cypressville, home of the nosiest, most loving people on earth. Get ready to have everyone know all your business, especially after you and Jenna make up and start dating." Jake winked at Ben and with a smile he said, "That girl is the biggest gossip in this town."

Ben wanted to tell Jake that if he patched things up with Jenna, he felt their personal life would always remain private unless they decided to spread the news. Jenna may come off as the town's busybody, but he knew her well enough to know that she was the best secret-keeper when she needed to be. Not a single person in this town had ever guessed that they were a couple before or had been seeing each other lately. The only ones who knew were those closest to Jenna.

Obviously, the things she gossips about are things people want others to know. Jenna was just blessed with a good nature and the ability to talk to anyone. People naturally tell her things once they know her. He knew this from past experience. She was the best listener when she wasn't being stubborn as hell.

Jake sat back down next to Melissa. He whispered in her ear as Ben started walking away. "Ben, wait." Melissa said. Ben turned back toward Melissa as she excused herself from the ice rink couple. "Thank you so much for everything." She gave him a hug.

Ben smiled. "You're welcome, it was my pleasure. You and Jake are like family."

Melissa pulled back and gave him a friendly kiss on the cheek. "I hope your parents are alright." She turned to Jake and her smile became radiant and her essence glowed in happiness.

He decided to take Jake's advice and ask Max and Walter if they'd seen her, but when he turned to where they had been moments ago, they too had disappeared.

After a few more minutes of looking for her, his phone buzzed in his pocket. It was his dad again.

"Get your butt over here, son, and get your mother and I out of this hospital. You know I hate these places."

"Fine, Dad, I was just telling Jake goodbye." Ben glanced at his watch. "I'll be there in forty minutes or so, if traffic is good."

He hung up the phone, disheartened that he couldn't find Jenna, he took off.

CHAPTER TWENTY-SIX

*S*tanding at the altar that close to Ben and not being able to talk to him was more stressful than anything Jenna had ever experienced. She was ready to bare her soul and trust him. Her heart melted as his eyes teared up when Melissa and Jake shared their vows. It was attractive that he cared so much for them. To Jenna, a man who wasn't afraid of his emotions was a big turn-on.

Ben must have felt her staring and glanced her way. His grin grew wide and her heart raced as she smiled back. She was glad she came to her senses and sort of apologized. She couldn't wait to get him alone and once and for all settle this estrangement she had caused. How had she ever doubted him? She let her petty fears stand in the way. The Ben she knew in the past, the Ben she recently rediscovered, and the Ben her best friend knew wasn't a liar. He was a man of integrity, a man who wore his heart on his sleeve, and a man that she knew with one hundred percent of her heart that she loved.

Having figured this out, she could finally breathe again. She clapped and cried when Melissa and Jake kissed and the pastor pronounced them man and wife. Jenna and Ben walked down the aisle but neither said a word. But he reassuringly squeezed her hand that was linked in the crook of his elbow with his other hand. Once they were out of the church, Blair was standing there like a predator waiting for her prey.

Jenna stared at her viciously and mouthed, "Don't mess with my man."

Blair's brows creased ever so slightly then Jenna pulled Ben away. Whether she got the message or not Jenna didn't know, but she would make sure when they got to the reception that Blair learned not to mess with her and the man of her dreams.

When Jenna arrived at the reception, the bridal party was rushed away for photos. She and Ben only got to have a couple of shared looks before she spotted her mom and dad enter the reception. She snuck away and hurried to meet them.

"You made it! Melissa will be so happy."

Her mom and dad exchanged hugs with Jenna.

Jenna's mother, Moreen, gave her dad a severe glance. "We would have made the actual wedding if your father didn't rip his good slacks in the gas station restroom. We had to stop at a retail store to buy him a new pair."

Her mother turned to Jenna's dad. "This is why you need to tell Uncle Max that he needs to give you at least two pairs of slacks to match these suit jackets, David." She then turned back to Jenna. "The color is near impossible to match. Thank goodness it's dark in here and no one will be able to tell."

David rolled his eyes at his wife and made a puppet with his hand, opening and closing its mouth, mocking her diatribe. Jenna laughed and her mom caught him and swatted his hand down.

"Seriously." Jenna glared at them both. "You two are horrible."

Jenna hugged her mom. "You worry too much. It's alright. You can't even notice and I doubt Max will be able to tell."

Max had walked up behind her. "Tell what?"

Moreen sighed, Jenna snickered and tattled on her dad. "Dad ripped his pants."

Max chuckled. "Pray tell, David, how did this happen? Because I know that there is no way the stitching was weak."

David's cheeks turned scarlet even in the low lighting. "This is neither the time nor the place for me to tell this tale."

Moreen started to laugh and David joined in.

Eventually, Moreen wiped her eyes. "Oh, I cannot wait for you to hear this story, but your dad is right, it's neither the time nor the place."

David grabbed his wife's hand and brought it up to his mouth and kissed it. Then he said to Jenna, "Sweetheart, you look beautiful and you outdid yourself with not only your gown but Melissa's as well. Excuse your mother and me while we go give her our best wishes."

Jenna smiled and turned to Max once they were gone. "I wonder how he split his pants."

Max chuckled. "Lord knows, but I am looking forward to finding out later."

Max and Jenna continued talking for a few minutes when Blair approached them. "There you two are, I have been looking for you." She had her phone on a selfie stick and stood between them.

Jenna tried to leave but Blair grabbed at her arm so roughly that her fingernails almost clawed into her skin. "Not so fast," she said with a fake laugh. "You and Max promised me a chat after the dress reveal, and as I'm leaving in a few minutes I need to get these videos made."

Jenna sighed. "Alright."

Blair turned to Max and he nodded.

"Wonderful, let's get started."

Blair pressed record.

"Hello, my beautiful followers. Wasn't the wedding simply charming? Now that you've seen the reception hall, I finally have our celebrity of the night with me, Maximilian Thorne, and his niece." Blair turned to Max. "Tell me, Max, you don't mind if I call you Max, do you?" She laughed in a haughty way.

"Only my close friends call me Max. I prefer Maximilian."

"Ah, yes." She cleared her throat with a bit of a frown but her artificial smile returned quickly. "Maximilian, tell me, what inspired you to branch out of men's fashion finally and create the most stunning wedding gown of the decade?"

She then turned to the screen as if her viewers were right there with her. "Don't you all agree!"

Blair turned back to Max before he could respond. "You better get ready because I know many women who follow me will be busting down your door for their very own gown." She turned her head back to the camera and nodded. "Am I right?"

Max caught Jenna's eye and raised his eyebrow and tilted his nose slightly toward the video screen as if pointing. Jenna knew what he was asking, whether she was really ready for all the attention. She had already decided that she wasn't going to hide anymore and nodded.

Max grinned wide and placed his hand on Blair's shoulder, making her selfie stick wiggle slightly. "Darling, I hate to break it to you and the world but I didn't design the gown. The only thing I did was help my beautiful niece sew on the pearls.'

Blair's mouth dropped open and Max turned to the screen and put his face in front of Blair's so that the viewers would only see him. "World, may I introduce to you the next great designer of—" He moved from taking up the whole screen and turned to Blair. "What was it? Ah yes, the decade."

He nudged Blair's arm holding the selfie stick, moving it toward Jenna. "This, darling, is the designer and seamstress of Melissa's wedding gown. I introduce to you, Jenna Thorne."

Max gave Jenna a kiss on the cheek and took the opportunity to bolt. Jenna tried to go after him but Blair clasped her wrist preventing her from leaving.

"Jenna Thorne, you are one sneaky woman. Why did you keep this a secret?"

For the next half-hour, Jenna suffered through answering all sorts of questions from Blair about the dress, her monogram shop, if she was going to design more gowns, and then, out of the blue, Paul showed up wearing a tux, followed by a few film crew members. Suddenly he was on one knee in front of Blair, and Blair transformed from aristocratic influencer to a woman who couldn't hide her true happiness at seeing the man she loved approach. This reinforced to Jenna that her delusions earlier were just that — jealousy and lack of confidence. It was obvious now that she wasn't interested in Ben other than just flirting with a good-looking man. "Paul, you made it."

Paul smiled, then pulled a small black box out of his coat pocket and got on one knee. Blair had her hand to her mouth and tears were filling her eyes. Jenna could clearly see this was a complete surprise.

They had three camera men filming and the one that was doing the live with her was getting closer to get Blair's reactions as she accepted Paul's proposal. Paul placed the huge diamond on her finger as she started crying and laughing with joy. Jenna had never seen someone cry so prettily in her life. Blair put her hand with the ring up to the camera and squeed then turned to Jenna, grabbing her arm again just as firmly as earlier so she couldn't escape.

"Jenna, with all the world as my witness, would you do me the honor of allowing me to be your second bride and design my gown?"

Jenna wanted to puke. She didn't like Blair, but there was no way she could say no when Blair had the entire world watching her YouTube channel live.

"I'd be honored."

Blair smiled and gave her a hug. Both actually seemed genuine. Guilt flooded Jenna, making her wonder if her feelings toward Blair were just tainted. Maybe this was how Melissa felt when Blair talked her way into coming to the wedding. Whatever it was, it was too late now. She was designing the woman's gown.

Jenna mumbled to herself, "I guess I'm in business." Then walked away as Blair concluded her live stream.

When she made her way back inside, she finally started to search for Ben. It was time she and he talked. She searched for him for a while before finally spotting Jake talking to Walter.

"Hey Jake, have you seen Ben?"

"Sorry, Jenna. Ben had to leave, I'm not sure when he's coming back."

Before she could ask more, Melissa came up to her and gave her a hug. "Thanks for everything, Jenna. You helped make tonight perfect." She then turned to Jake. A radiant smile graced her lips and her eyes shone with love for him.

"It's time to go."

Jake grabbed Melissa's hand and they walked off.

Walter held his elbow out to Jenna for her to hold. "Well, hun, let's go find your folks and that uncle of yours. I think it's time we all head home. We have a big day tomorrow."

"What's going on tomorrow?"

"The cleaning up of this place. I have a buyer interested and have to have it ready for them."

"But I thought Melissa hired a clean-up crew."

"She did but they backed out at the last minute. She gave them my number and I didn't have the heart to tell her. So, I decided to arrange some volunteers tonight. Everyone is meeting here tomorrow at eight."

"Well, in that case, I guess we better go."

As they walked out Jenna searched the practically empty building for Ben one last time, knowing that Jake wouldn't have lied, but she had hoped that Ben would come back for her.

CHAPTER TWENTY-SEVEN

*W*aking up the next morning was hard. Jenna had cried herself to sleep, mad at herself because she wanted to talk to Ben so badly but once more didn't have his number. All night she prayed he'd be at the clean-up but he never showed.

She called the B and B asking Jane if she had his number, but Jane wouldn't give out any of her clients' information, even if they did know one another, and recommended she call Melissa or Jake instead. Jenna thanked her, feeling disheartened but at the same time glad to know Jane's level of professionalism.

Jenna hated bothering Melissa on her honeymoon but was so desperate that she did it anyway. Her call went straight to voicemail. She sent a text but it never changed to "read." She didn't have Jake's number so when she got to work she decided to keep the shop closed a little longer and made her way to Susan's boutique, Susu's Petal.

Jenna took a deep breath to calm her nerves, praying Susan wouldn't judge her too much.

The little bell above the door chimed and Susan came out of the back office. "Hey Jenna, can I help you find something?"

"Hey Susan, um..." Jenna shivered as a chill came over her. Her stomach started to churn and her mouth dried out. Darkness started to close in around her and her breathing got louder in her ears.

Susan rushed to Jenna's side, grabbing her elbow and walking her to a stool near her register. "Honey, are you okay? You need me to call your mom to get you?"

Jenna tried to take a deep breath but instead broke down in tears. Embarrassed but unable to stop, she covered her face with her hands.

Susan started rubbing her back with one hand. "Hey, it will be okay." Jenna felt Susan step away and within seconds she felt some tissue being tucked under her fingertips. Jenna moved her hands and hung on to the Kleenex, blew her nose, and wiped her eyes.

"I'm so embarrassed," Jenna moaned. "I think the stress of everything happening over the past few weeks just got to me all of a sudden. And when you asked if I needed help finding something, which I do, just—" She blew her nose again.

"Nothing in my shop."

Jenna looked apologetically at Susan. She glanced guiltily at the sunshine umbrella that she never purchased. "I mean, not that I don't love the inventory you have, but it's not really what I need or want, ugh that sounded so wrong — it's just that all the stress from over the past few days just got too much and I let it all out without meaning to. Oh man, I'm rambling and I know this doesn't make any sense. I'm so sorry I broke down on you."

Susan pulled another stool up next to Jenna and sat on it, then placed her hand on Jenna's knee, reminding Jenna of her mom when she was about to have a serious talk with her. "Look, Jenna, we all have these moments. It's nothing to be ashamed of, and you and I are like family now, so think of me as another sister. If you want to talk about whatever it is that's bothering you, I am here."

Jenna started crying and hugged Susan. "I just need a hug for a second." Then she laughed. "I feel so ridiculously childish."

Susan chuckled and hugged her. "Childishness isn't always a bad thing, Jenna. Why don't you tell me what's got you thinking that?"

Jenna moved out of the hug and wiped her eyes again. "I fell in love." Then she laughed and said, "Susan, I fell in love with the same man twice!"

Susan joined in the laughter. "There is nothing wrong with falling in love, I hope to do the same again too, just not with my first love." She winked. "My ex is not the most reliable, nor the best communicator, so I don't want a repeat of that marriage. I want someone who will be expressive with his words and actions and always be there for me and Megan in the future." Susan sighed. "But this isn't about me." Her eyes brightened and she sat up, scooting to the edge of her seat. "Tell me, who's this mystery man?"

Jenna tucked her head down. Lifting her eyes to look at Susan from below her bangs, she whispered, "Ben."

Susan gasped and clapped. "Best man Ben?"

Jenna nodded and Susan stood up and gave Jenna a hug. "Oh, I'm so happy for you. Ben is amazing. Why didn't I see before that you two are perfect for one another?"

Jenna couldn't help but smile as Susan's excitement mixed with her own at finally admitting out loud, she loved Ben. "Melissa and Jake thought so too. For months they had been trying to set us up on a date of sorts before we met for the wedding, but somehow it never worked. But that isn't the crazy thing."

Susan sat down again, then stood up and walked over to the door and put the closed sign up. "This sounds like a good story and it's close enough to lunch for a break."

Jenna laughed, looking at her watch. "It's only nine-thirty, you just opened."

"Ah pfft, it's a Monday. It's usually slow anyway. Plus, I need another romance to focus on since my love life is dead."

She scooted her stool closer and motioned with her hand. "Carry on."

Jenna chuckled under her breath. "Promise you won't tell anyone what I'm about to tell you, or at least not until I talk to Melissa."

Susan sat up straight. "I don't really need to know, Jenna. You can talk to Mel first."

Jenna gave her a grateful smile. "I know I could, but I decided recently that I was going to make some changes in my life, and talking about this right now with you feels right for some reason. But I would really appreciate it if you could keep it to yourself until I can talk to Melissa. I am hoping to talk to her within the first few days of her coming home."

"Got it." Susan made a zip movement with her fingers over her lips. "I will wait for you to tell me you told her before I tell the Cypressville Gazette."

Jenna laughed. "Yes, I'd appreciate it." She rubbed her palms on her denim clad thighs. "Ben and I met when I was nineteen and living in New York with Max. We dated for about five months and fell in love really quick, but I was stupid back then."

Jenna went through the entire tale of her relationship and her game-playing with Ben, and even her jealousy over Blair, who ended up not even being interested in him. Blair had DM'd her on Instagram after her interview at the reception, thanking her for taking her on as a client and giving Jenna her phone number. She then went on to apologize for the miscommunication about Ben being her escort and explained that she seriously wasn't interested in him and that Paul was her one true love. She didn't like upsetting fans, and Ben's mother was terribly sweet, and Blair didn't see any harm in accepting the invitation for a ride to the reception, knowing Paul couldn't be there.

Susan listened raptly, asking a few questions here and there when the timeline jumped in Jenna's rendition. Finally, at the end of the conversation, she said, "Jenna, I wish I had his number or address because I would sure give it to you if I did. I'm so sorry I couldn't be of more help. The good news is this won't be like when you were younger because you can get his number from Jake when they get back from their honeymoon and you can call him and tell him all this yourself."

"Thank you so much for listening. It feels like the biggest weight has been lifted off my shoulders. After I straighten things out with Ben, I'm going to tell Melissa first then my family not only my greatest secret but also that I've finally overcome my insecurities over becoming a designer."

Susan stood up so fast her stool toppled back. "Are you saying what I think you're saying?"

"Yep." Jenna smiled. "I am going to start making my designs and selling them."

"Wait, how will this work with Ben? He and his dad own a publishing company and I can't imagine Ben being able to move with you to New York and keep running their business. Oh, Jenna, what will you do?"

Jenna looked at her seriously. "I've thought about that too when I was struggling to sleep, and Max and I talked about it. Max is retiring and moving here to Cypressville. I don't want to go big, but I wouldn't mind people knowing of me. Maybe being introduced to some of his friends to get a trunk show or something. But he believes that a designer can work anywhere they please and Cypressville is just as good as anywhere else. We already put a call in this morning for the new contractor who moved into town to give us a bid on redesigning the shop."

"What new contractor? If you hire him let me know if he's any good. My house is forty years old and starting to have some issues, if I ever need one, it would be nice to have a list ready."

"His name is TJ. Remind me to send you his contact info when I get back to my shop."

"Sure, so back to you and Ben. How will that work with you turning your shop into a dress shop? Which I think is fantastic, by the way."

A bubble of excitement flooded Jenna every time she thought about the dress shop. Funny how she had been so afraid of designing because she assumed she would have to fill Max's shoes somehow, move to New York, and live his life. But that wasn't true. It was something Ben had said while watching her fix a hem on the gown that made her think.

He'd sat back on her pink settee, making it look smaller than usual, and all he said was, and told her she should enlarge the shop and make a design studio. "I'm sure people would love to get bridal gowns from a quaint little boutique town," he'd said, and gave her the card of a building contractor who'd just moved to town.

Jenna turned back to Susan. "Honestly, Ben is the one who recommended I redesign my space. Max walked in as he was finishing the comment and we all sat down and talked about it for a while. Max wants to work there and have the next reality TV show about a small-town boutique with him as the host, to, of course, keep me out of the spotlight, as per my request. He'd like to help the ladies find the perfect gown for their big day, and if he's feeling so inclined, he may design a suit or two for the groom."

"Wow, just wow. I can see that happening. Max is well known and last year's sexiest model over sixty. I can't imagine any network turning that down. You'll make our town even more famous than the influencers last Christmas. Should I start increasing my inventory?"

Jenna snorted. "Girl, we haven't even opened a shop yet. Don't start spending more money than you can make. But to answer your earlier question about me and Ben, I would move to him in a heartbeat if I had to. I can design dresses anywhere with a notepad and come to town when needed. It's only a few hours away and Max will always be here. He is selling his place in Manhattan to move in with Walter."

"Wait, slow down, Max and Walter are an item?"

"It seems like secrets and past loves run in the family. Because Walter and Max were an item in the eighties before Max became famous. He ran away only to find his way back home thirty years later and Walter, bless his heart, was still waiting for him."

"Oh, my goodness, that is so heartbreaking and sweet at the same time."

"I know. Fortunately, it only took me eight years to reconcile my love. At least with myself. Now I have to find Ben and tell him."

"Don't worry, you will. Jenna, I just want you to know that I'm really proud of you for recognizing your faults and rising above them. I wish I had done that in the past, and although I did finally start living my dream it took me much longer to figure it out."

"Susan, you aren't much older than me."

"Nearly five years, but it feels a lot older."

"Well, it isn't, so hush." Jenna stood up. "Thanks for listening but I have to go open my shop, and it appears you have a customer lurking at the window wondering why you are closed."

They both walked to the door. As Jenna left, Susan welcomed the lurker into her shop.

CHAPTER TWENTY-EIGHT

*J*t had been two weeks since Melissa's wedding and Jenna practically bounced in her seat at Main Street Java as she waited for Melissa to meet her for coffee.

Walter came up behind Jenna and placed his hand on her shoulder, making her jump. "Oh, Walter, I'm sorry."

"Sugar, you need to calm down. Melissa will think I gave you too much coffee and she might cut you off."

Jenna laughed. "I'm just nervous to tell her and anxious to get Ben's number."

"What? have you been waiting all this time for Ben's phone number?"

"Yes, why?"

"Sugar, I have Ben's number. I could have given it to you."

"Walter!" Jenna practically shouted and gave him a look of incredulity. "How did you not know? Ben has been all I've talked about to you and Max, and my parents, and on the phone with Leigh Anne for nearly two weeks."

Walter gave her a sad smile. "Honey, I'm so sorry! I wish I would have thought to give it to you but it never entered my mind. I guess I was just thinking you wanted to talk to Melissa first to rectify the situation before you talked to Ben in person. Honestly, I'm surprised he isn't back yet. He made it sound like he wouldn't stay gone too long last time I talked to him."

"Walter, have you talked to Ben recently?"

"Well not since you've been going on and on about him. If I had, I would have told him you wanted to talk to him."

Jenna folded her arms and pouted, leaning back in her chair. "Walter, I'm so upset with you."

Melissa arrived at that moment. "Uh oh, Walter. What did you do, run out of coffee?"

Jenna gave Walter an intense stare, hoping he got the hint to leave. Jenna laughed. "No, it's something completely different." Jenna stood up to give Melissa a hug.

"Welcome home, Mrs. Blessing."

Melissa's grin spread wide. "I don't think I will ever get tired of hearing that."

The ladies both sat down and Walter brought over Melissa's favorites.

"Thank you, Walter."

"You're welcome. You girls enjoy your chat."

Melissa took a sip of her mocha latte. "So, tell me all the juicy gossip that's been going on while I was gone."

Jenna gave a strained laugh and Melissa's brow arched over her cup of coffee.

"Jenna, what in the world are you hiding? I know that sound. You are embarrassed about something. Better spit it out before it eats you up. You know I won't judge."

"I know." Jenna took a sip of her coffee. "It's just hard." Jenna sighed and took a deep breath.

Melissa pulled Snickerdoodle out of the bag where she had been napping and held her close. "Jenna, you're making me worried. Are you okay? Did I do something wrong?"

Jenna hurriedly assured her. "No, you did nothing wrong, it was me. I'm a horrible friend."

"No, you aren't. What has got you thinking this?"

"Remember how I told you that I'd tell you all about my romance in New York when you got back?"

Melissa nodded. "I certainly hope you aren't beating yourself up over that. I can understand why you didn't want to talk about it. Believe me, if you weren't a witness to my high school drama with Jake, I may have very well kept that a secret from you too. Sometimes that's just easier."

Jenna gave her a sad smile. "This is what I love about you, Mel. You are always so quick to forgive and put yourself in others' shoes. But still, there's so much more to the story than you could imagine. No one knew anything about it until recently. Max and Walter figured it out the fastest and I only told my family about it in the past couple weeks."

"Girl, please spit it out. You're making me so crazy with curiosity. What don't I know?"

Jenna did what Mel requested and blurted out quickly, "Ben was the guy." She held her breath, gauging Melissa's reaction.

Melissa's eyes widened, her arms loosened, and she relaxed her grip from Snickerdoodle, then she burst out laughing.

Jenna blew out her breath. "That is not the reaction I was expecting."

Melissa started laughing harder.

"Why is this so funny? I don't think it's funny, Mel."

Melissa tried to catch her breath. "I'm so sorry. The way you were acting made me expect something tragic or horrible, and to find out it was Ben all along, what a small frickin' world! And all this time Jake and I were trying to set y'all up. How in the world did y'all keep this quiet? Both of you are good actors. I would never have guessed he was the one that broke your heart."

Melissa paused, then all of a sudden, her tone changed. "I am so mad at him." She held Snickerdoodle over the table and silently encouraged Jenna to take her. After Jenna grabbed the dog, Melissa pulled out her phone, opening the screen.

"I'm so mad I could spit. How dare he show up here and give you the cold shoulder? I'm going to give him a piece of my mind."

Jenna hurriedly swiped the phone out of Melissa's hand and hung up when she heard Ben answer. "Don't you dare! Oh my gosh. It wasn't his fault, it was all mine."

The phone rang with Ben's face and name popping up. "Please tell him it was a butt dial, then I will explain."

Melissa huffed then answered, "Hey Ben, sorry about the butt dial." She paused, then smiled. "Yes, the honeymoon was amazing, and both Jake and I appreciate you being sneaky, upgrading our room, and having champagne and strawberries waiting for us."

Jenna listened in and her heart melted at not only how thoughtful but how generous Ben was. That was an incredible gift. Melissa paused again. Jenna could hear the deep tone of Ben's voice but not his words. She couldn't wait to see him again.

"Yes, you're right, the view was beautiful." Melissa's eyes lit up and she grinned mischievously "Is that so? I didn't know the specifics." She glanced at Jenna, her grin widening so much her cheek made a little sound.

Jenna mouthed, "What?"

Melissa shook her head, still speaking to Ben. "Well, I mean Jake did mention it but I didn't really absorb the whole thing. I believe that will be amazing and I for one am very happy for you."

Melissa stopped talking and listened once more. She smiled and tilted her head side to side while making a puppet motion with her hand. "I'll make sure to tell Jake. Talk to you soon."

Jenna could barely contain herself. "What was that all about?"

"Oh, nothing really. So, tell me exactly and in detail how you met Ben and why on earth y'all broke up."

Jenna went through the entire tale again. Melissa groaned a few times throughout the story as Jenna told her about the game. When Jenna was done, Melissa exhaled as if exhausted. "I still can't believe that you and I are so much alike that we both tried to set up moments of serendipity with poor Ben. What a good sport he was!"

"I know! I was so mad at myself for so long."

"Jenna, you do know that Ben has never stopped loving you, right? He tells everyone about his lost love. I still can't believe it was you. I mean seriously, he never once used your name. You and your secrets. Girl, I knew I could trust you but heck now I know if I ever tell you to keep a secret you will. How in the world did everyone peg you as a blabbermouth gossip?" Melissa covered her mouth, her eyes widened.

"Hey! That's not nice."

They both started laughing. Melissa muttered under her breath, "But it's true."

Walter came by their table. "You two doing alright? Feel like spreading the joy?"

They both looked at Walter and started laughing more. Jenna pointed to Walter and burst out, "He's more of a gossip than I am!"

Walter brought his hand to his chest and feigned offense. "Moi?"

Melissa stuck up for Jenna as best friends do. "That's right! He's the one who told me about Dad and Andrea's wedding before they did."

"Now sugar, you promised you wouldn't hold that little slip against this old fragile soul."

Max's voice sounded from the entrance. "Now Walter, stop playing games, we all know you're one of the sturdiest seventy-five-year-olds in the area."

"Well, if Jake were here, he would take my side. That husband of yours sees my ladder out and insists I shouldn't climb it because he's scared, I'm going to fall."

Max, Melissa, and Jenna all said at the same time, "You shouldn't climb ladders!"

Walter gave them all a peeved glare. "See, old."

As they all chuckled, the bell on the door chimed.

"Hey Walter, I finally made it. Is the contractor here?"

Jenna froze. Max moved away from the table, making Jenna visible to Ben as he came through the door.

Ben and Jenna just stared at one another in silence.

Melissa got up quickly and Max and Walter both exclaimed they had to go.

Jenna stood. Mel hugged her goodbye and said, "Talk to Ben."

"I am determined to fix this, don't worry."

As Melissa walked out, she gave Ben a brief hug then rushed out the door.

Ben walked over to Jenna with his hands in his jeans pockets.

"Hey, I've wanted to come back sooner but things with my office, my parents, and my house took longer than expected. Do you have time to talk now?"

Jenna swallowed hard. Her heart raced with nerves and excitement. "Yes." Then she plopped back into her seat.

Ben sat where Melissa had vacated.

Neither one said anything for a while, then they started talking at the same time. They both chuckled in relief. Then Ben said, "You first."

Jenna took a deep breath, pulled out her phone, and said, "First things first, what is your phone number?"

Ben laughed, relieved, and gave her his number. It rang in his pocket. She smiled at him. "Now you have my number. I never want to go without speaking to you again. I am so sorry for all of my silliness. You were right. I needed to trust Melissa and I needed to stop playing games. I think I was just so scared of being used or hurt that I just couldn't stop."

Ben opened his mouth, about to interrupt.

"Please let me finish."

Ben closed his mouth and sat back to listen, but he put his hand on the table and opened it palm up and wiggled his fingers at her. Jenna smiled and took her hand off her lap to place in his. Ben sighed in what sounded like relief.

"Ben, I never should have doubted your character. I mean, if Jake and Mel loved you and wanted us to be together, I should have trusted that you hadn't changed. I trusted you back when we were in New York. I really did, but I was still so young and stupid and—"

Jenna was about to say more, but Ben did something completely unexpected. He leaned over the table and kissed her. She completely forgot what she was about to say, his lips were as soft and warm as she remembered, and before long she had her hands on his cheeks, keeping him close. They pulled apart when they both became aware of the claps and whistles coming from Max and Walter and a few of the staff and customers.

Jenna felt her cheeks turn scarlet and placed her hands over them to cool them down.

Ben's voice was a tone deeper, huskier, after the kiss. "Don't ever let me hear you say you are stupid. You are one of the most brilliant women I know. If I hear it again, I may just have to kiss the words right out of your mouth."

Jenna gave Ben a wicked smile and whispered teasingly, "Stupid."

Ben smiled and leaned over the table toward her again. Jenna laughed and put her hands on his shoulders, pushing him back down. "Okay, okay. I'll stop."

"Jenna, there is something I need to tell you. I hadn't quite planned to tell you here but now is as good a time as any, right?"

"I'd say so. This sounds serious, do I need to be worried?"

"I don't think so. I was worried but now I'm starting to feel a bit more confident."

"Well spill, I'm not good with waiting."

Ben laughed. "I think that is an understatement, but I digress. Jenna, I love you and—"

Jenna jumped up, not letting him finish what he was saying,

and leaped onto his lap, hugging him tightly. "I love you too!" Then she kissed him soundly on the lips. His hand went to her lower back, keeping her in place, and she smiled into his lips. She pulled back just enough to where their noses were still touching and said, "I really do love you with all my heart, Ben. I'm so sorry I was stupid."

"What did I say about that word?" he whispered back and kissed her once more.

Walter shouted across the cafe, "You two take it to the back." And he laughed.

Ben shifted Jenna off his lap and stood, grabbing her hand. "Actually, Walter, that is a good idea."

Shocked, Jenna looked around the cafe, a little freaked out that Ben was playing along.

"Walter, do you have the keys?"

Walter pulled some keys out of his register and handed them over to Ben. Jenna recognized the old-fashioned keyring as the ones for the space next door where they had Melissa's reception.

Ben led Jenna to the back room that connected the two buildings, unlocked the door, and let her into the large empty space. "What's going on, Ben? What are we doing in here?"

Ben stood with his arms wide, twisting from side to side. "This, Jenna, is the new home of Bayou Books and Sanderson Publishing. I bought this from Walter. I'm moving my family company here and opening a local bookstore."

Jenna was flabbergasted. Then Ben's words sunk in and she squealed and ran jumping into his arms, making him stumble a bit. He then swung her around just like he used to back in the day. He stopped and she slid down his body. "You're moving here?"

"Yes."

"Where are you going to live?"

"Temporarily at the B and B, then hopefully I can convert the large storage area upstairs into a small apartment. I've already hired TJ, the contractor.

"Me too!" Jenna squealed.

"What are you hiring him for?"

"When you were away, I went public as a designer and turned my shop into a bridal boutique. I am going to be designing bridal gowns and the occasional vintage dress. I even have my first client. Do you remember Blair?"

Ben nodded.

"Paul proposed to her in front of all her followers on a live stream at Melissa's wedding, and she hired me on the spot. She has already been texting me non-stop about her ideas and her wedding is a year away."

Ben picked Jenna up and swung her around again, then stopped and gave her another kiss. "I'm so proud of you."

Jenna looked up at Ben. "I am so happy you are moving here."

EPILOGUE

*O*ne month later.

Jenna pulled up to her shop, the sign she used to have stenciled on the front window saying Jenna's Monograms had been removed and was now covered with beautiful blush taffeta window drapings that were closed. Her new sign was in a large box inside, waiting to be opened and hung up today. Ben and TJ, the spitting image of Keanu Reeves, were standing in front drinking coffee while waiting for her.

"Good morning," she chirped, practically skipping in excitement. Both men smiled.

Ben greeted her with a hug and whispered into her neck. "Someone is happy this morning." Then kissed her cheek.

"Indeed I am. Where is Max? He should have been here by now."

TJ said, "He's coming, I see him now."

Jenna leaned around Ben to look down the sidewalk. Max waved. Jenna started bouncing on her toes. "I can't wait to see the sign up." She turned to TJ and poked his arm with her finger. "And you, mister, are a man of many talents. I swear the inside of my shop is absolutely beautiful and elegant and charming and everything I could have imagined. I can't believe you were able to finish the redesign so quickly."

TJ's grin grew wider as Jenna spoke. "Honestly, I haven't worked with my hands in so long that I think coming here and meeting you folks was a blessing in disguise. I think I found my passion again."

Jenna sighed and gave TJ a half hug. "Aww, TJ, I'm so glad you came here too."

Ben chimed in, "Me too, man." Then he glanced at Jenna. She caught his eyes and he lifted his brow and did one of his cute little nods, then tilted his head as he tried to communicate a question. Jenna squinted her eyes at him, trying to figure out what he was trying to get across to her. Then he tilted his head toward TJ, then again toward the direction of the old warehouse. Then her eyes lit up with insight and she nodded.

Ben turned back to TJ, who was looking at them as if they were nuts. TJ chuckled. "You guys are so cute, trying to silently talk to one another. If you are aiming to try and be discrete," his hand clamped on Ben's shoulder, shaking it gently, "I'm sorry to tell you, you need a heck of a lot more practice."

Ben playfully swiped TJ's hand off his shoulder. "If you're going to be rude then I guess I won't offer you my apartment to move into since Jenna insisted, we make her house, our house."

TJ stepped back, his eyes widened. "What? Are you serious?"

Ben winked at Jenna and she grabbed his hand. Before any more could be said, Max walked up. "What are you darlings doing loitering on the sidewalk? We are supposed to be unveiling the signage."

Jenna dropped Ben's hand and clapped and bounced up and down like a kid on Christmas morning before she hurriedly pulled her keys out of her jeans pocket. The bell chimed as they all crossed the threshold of the new store.

Max came up beside Jenna. "So, darling, let's get this box

opened. I'm anxious to see which name you ended up choosing for the boutique."

Ben handed Jenna a box cutter and she began slicing the cardboard. The front of the box fell open and they all stepped back. She removed the vine-like wrought iron hanging bracket then started ripping the sheet of foam off. "My goodness, they got this on good. Can you guys hold this up for me while I get the foam off?"

Ben and TJ stepped forward to hold the sign as Jenna tore off the foam wrapper. Once she had most of it loose, the men set the sign back down, leaning it against the wall. The sign was a simple blush-colored oval with the name in gold lettering, Love by Design.

Max walked up to Jenna and leaned down to kiss her head. "It's perfect, darling. Now the fun begins."

The End

GALETTE DES ROIS

A FRENCH KING CAKE

This traditional French dessert is very popular at Chez François. When François was a young boy living in Normandy, France, he could always be found at his mother's side making this dessert for the Epiphany. The Epiphany is a Christian holiday celebrating the day the three kings gave their gifts to the newborn king, baby Jesus. Galette (pancake) des Rois (king) generally has a little fève (bean) baked into the filling and whoever gets the slice with the bean gets to be king/queen for the day. In Southern Louisiana, you will find several variations of king cake, generally with a little plastic baby to hide inside, available during the Carnival season, which begins on the Epiphany.

When François moved to Louisiana he was thrilled to find such a large French community that welcomed him and his French cuisine. His Galette de Rois is a favorite in the region that people enjoy until Mardi Gras.

Keep reading to learn how to make Galette des Rois.

Ingredients:

Almond Cream Filling:

- ½ cup almond meal or almond flour
- ¼ cup granulated sugar
- 1 large egg
- 3 tablespoons butter, softened
- ⅜ teaspoon almond extract
- ½ teaspoon ground cinnamon — Optional
- ½ orange zest – Optional
- 1 tablespoon all-purpose flour

Cake:

- 17 ounces store-bought puff pastry sheets, thawed
- 1 fève (dried bean) or whole almond, optional
- 1 large egg, beaten
- 2 tablespoons confectioners sugar

Steps:

Creating the Almond Cream

1. Gather the ingredients.
2. Combine almond meal, sugar, egg, softened butter, almond extract, (ground cinnamon and/or orange zest are optional), and flour in the bowl of a food processor.
3. Blend to a smooth, creamy paste. Feel free to make this cream a few days in advance, then refrigerate in an airtight container.

Assembling the Cake

1. Gather the ingredients.
2. Preheat oven to 425 F. Line a baking sheet with parchment paper.
3. Roll out sheets of puff pastry and cut out 2 (11-inch) circles. Place the first disc on a prepared baking sheet, and spread an even layer of almond cream, leaving a 1-inch border around the edges.
4. If you wish to include a fève, you can do so at this point. Simply nestle it in the almond cream.
5. Place second puff pastry disc on top of the filling, and crimp edges with a fork to seal cake.
6. Using a sharp knife, score a decorative pattern into the top layer of pastry without cutting through to the almond filling. Brush galette with beaten egg (this will create a golden crust).

Baking the Cake

1. Bake cake for 15 minutes. Remove from oven and dust cake with powdered sugar.
2. Return to oven and bake for an additional 10 to 12 minutes, until puff pastry becomes a deep golden brown. Allow cake to cool for 20 minutes.

Note:

- The almond paste can be made ahead of time up to three days and stored in an airtight container and placed in the refrigerator.
- This dessert is best eaten the same day as the crust can

become soggy, but if there are leftovers wrap them in plastic wrap and they can be stored for up to two days.

- If you tuck a bean or whole almond into the filling make sure to warn your guest or any children. It could be a choking hazard.
- For those with nut allergies, you can substitute the almond meal with regular flour and the almond extract with ¾ tsp vanilla extract.
- If you would like to alter the recipe to make a vegan version, substitute puff pastry to a vegan brand and vegan butter. For the egg in the filling you can use 1tbsp ground flaxseed plus 3tbsp water (let sit for five minutes until thickened). The egg wash can be substituted with aquafaba for a good shine and golden crust, if you don't have that on hand you can use coconut oil.
- Also, if you want to keep with tradition, have a crown around for the finder of the fève to receive and be the king/queen of the day.

Enjoy!

ACKNOWLEDGMENTS

To Karri and Sarah, thank you for always being there to support, encourage, promote, and keep me focused on the end goal. Your friendship, time, and support mean the world to me. To my sister Bernie, my forever first reader, knowing you loved this book as much as my first book every step of the way gave me hope that others would find the same kind of happiness you did. To my two beautiful daughters who believe in my dreams just as much as I do. You both mean the world to me, and I appreciate your love, loyalty, and ever-present support always. To Elizabeth, my best friend and chosen sister, thank you for helping to develop my imagination my entire life. To everyone who has listened to me endlessly talk about my book and characters, you all are the absolute best.

ABOUT THE AUTHOR

Kristen Tassin is an emerging author of small-town contemporary romance. Kristen is in love with love. Ever since she was a young girl, she dreamed of the happily ever after. Kristen has always wanted to be a writer but never attempted until after her two beautiful daughters were grown. Living down south, where the heat is heavy and humid, Kristen tends to spend most days inside where the air is cool, reading a good book, or pretending winter is near watching Christmas romance movies on her favorite network. Now, she spends her free time drinking coffee and weaving her very own dreams into stories. This book is the second of many to come featuring the small southern town of Cypressville. For more information on current and future books you can find Kristen on social media, or you can sign up for her newsletter on her website kristentassin.com

facebook.com/author.kristentassin

instagram.com/kristentassin.author

tiktok.com/kristentassin.author

goodreads.com/kristen_tassin

amazon.com/~/e/B0982VMXZV

ALSO BY KRISTEN TASSIN

Christmas in Cypressville

Coming Soon
Love Under Construction

The Cypressville Gazette

Weekly Edition

Volume CXIX, No.6,172   Cypressville, Sunday, September 5, 2021 $1.25

LOVE BY DESIGN

NOW OPEN

TRUNK SHOW

WITH

JENNA THORNE

Time To Fall In Love

By Joanie Hill

Local Jenna Thorne has helped put Cypressville on the map once more since designing the stunningly exquisite wedding gown for Melissa Albright's wedding this past June. Cypressville was shocked when Maximillian Thorne, the famous fashion designer, and Jenna's uncle, revealed to the internet fans of YouTube and TikTok influencer Blair Kincaid that he did not design Melissa's gown as speculated, but it was his niece's design. During the live stream from the wedding reception, Miss Kincaid got a surprise of her own. Paul Simineaux proposed to her. A beaming Blair turned immediately to Jenna and asked her on the spot to design her wedding gown.

Continued on page 3, column 1

All Photos By Judy Chaudoir

Cypressville Gazette

Weather

Sunday, 5 September

Night +79° Day +90° Mostly clear

Monday, 6 September

Night +81° Day +81° Partly cloudy and brief rain..

Tuesday, 7 September

Night +77° Day +86° Partly cloudy

Wednesday, 8 September

Night +75° Day +88° Mostly cloudy

Thursday, 9 September

Night +77° Day +88° Clear

Friday, 10 September

Night +70° Day +84° Clear

Saturday, 11 September

Night +68° Day +84° Clear

Dow Jones

Petering Out
S&P 500, Dow Jones Industrial Average extend drop from all-time highs

The Tattle Tales

By Madame LaRue

For those longing for some juice, I just overheard on the grapevine that one of our newly married couples is expecting their first child. I won't give names just yet, but since there are only three newlyweds in town, I'll let you try to figure it out for yourself.

Mr. Fournier and Mr. Dorsey, both 79 years young, are in competition again. They're betting on who can last the longest standing in front of their respective stores next week before one of them needs a chair. Who do you think will win? Cast your bet at Main Street Java before Sunday, September 12.

Opening, Summer 2022

Bott Sanderson

Cypressville Gazette

Continued From
Page One

Miss Thorne agreed to be Miss Kincaid's designer with little hesitation. In the last two months, *Jenna's Monograms*, located on Main Street, has been renovated by construction newcomer TJ Gatz and renamed *Love by Design*. The soft opening went off with a bang on August 4th. After the opening, during our interview, Jenna gave a sneaky smile, admitting she received a request to design a gown for a well-known-celebrity friend of her uncle. We at the Cypressville Gazette wonder if this celebrity might choose to have their wedding in our little boutique town. Hint, hint Jenna.

With the success of *Love by Design's* soft opening, Miss Thorne has been busy. She has created several gowns to be seen in her first trunk show this Saturday, September 11.

Love by Design will be open from 10-4. In addition, there will be a fashion runway at 2 pm introducing her fall collection of cocktail attire and wedding gowns. Fashion designer Maximilian Thorne will escort each lucky model.

Maximilian Thorne

New York Fashion Designer/Model retires to Cypressville. Although Mr. Thorne has announced his retirement, he plans to continue designing tuxedos for select clientele of *Love by Design*. Rumor has it he is in talks with a major television network interested in developing a reality show focusing on small town designers.